MedPal: The end of the world, or the beginning?

by Cynthia Schaefer

https://www.flurbanparadise.com

Find me on Amazon:

https://www.amazon.com/stores/author/B09P9MH

HX4/about

Publisher: Flurban Paradise

4786 SW 72nd Ave.

Davie, Florida 33314

https://www.flurbanparadise.com1

https://www.facebook.com/Flurbanparadise

https://www.instagram.com/flurban_paradise/

https://www.linkedin.com/in/cynthia-schaefer-

a1442a97/

Preface: The AI Accords

In 2028, a world devasted by a cyber war made a desperate decision. One hundred and seventeen countries agreed to binding arbitration by AI to stop the war. AI was the ultimate incorruptible mediator. The decisions made were based on the highest good for the entire planet. None of the parties were happy with the results, but all complied. Countries had their laws changed, populations moved, and borders altered.

The accords also addressed the use of AI. The accords were over three hundred pages, but there were two overarching themes:

1.)   AI as a tool cannot be used in any manner that is not meant to better the conditions of mankind.

2.)   The use of AI in any creation must be disclosed.

Industries disappeared, and new ones arose. AI was kept in check by the Global Accord Peacekeepers, and the fragile new world moved forward.

Chapter 1: Jared

The rising sun glinted off the sleek, glass walls of Eos' headquarters. The solar arrays turned toward the beams in unison, like children lifting their faces to the sun.

Jared Muzos stood at his corner office window, watching the drones moving through the city. They darted and swooped like swallows after mosquitos as they avoided each other, carrying everything from groceries to whatever people ordered from Walmazon, the only surviving retail company.

People quickly stopped caring about monopolies when systems were broken, and there was only one option to fill the gaps. It didn't take much for ideals to fall when the Grim Reaper was outside your door.

The headache that had been pounding all morning increased its relentless throb as he looked down on the few people on the streets below. Some walked, but most glided on hovers, surfing the air inches above the sidewalk. The streets were still mostly empty, and he could imagine tumbleweeds blowing through the vast, desolate roads like some old western ghost town.

In the distance, a flock of drones rises from a Walmazon hub. They emerge en masse from the center of the warehouse, an ominous metal cloud, and explode out in all directions like the old cluster fireworks. They feel like war.

A headline scrolled by on the building opposite his. *Bitcoin hits $175,873.* Underneath that, the population clock ticker streamed the endless bad news of deaths without births.

He was one of the lucky ones. He was alive and had a mission and meaning in his life. The AI Accords had reformed their world in every way possible. When thirty percent of the world population died within twenty-one months, your priorities shifted.

The Accords were bold and wide-reaching. The world had seen enough suffering, and everyone was ready for peace. The Accords had passed almost overnight. The U.N. became the GAP- Global Accord Peacekeepers.

Universal Basic Income. No more fossil fuels. World peace. A minimum standard of living for all. Lofty goals for a world that had almost imploded. AI solved a lot of mankind's problems at record speed. But at what cost?

The deadly pandemic had come first. The Crush variant caused airways to swell. Without a ventilator, chances of survival were slim. The hospitals had been overwhelmed.

Then came the Cyber War. Over a billion people died while governments and terrorist groups hacked each other, taking down power grids, transportation networks, and healthcare systems. It was the quickest and deadliest world war in history.

As the world crumbled overnight, institutions that had existed for centuries fell with hardly a whimper. Eos had formed from the ashes of the once great tech companies like Apple, Microsoft, Google, and Meta. Like many of his peers, Jared found himself with enormous responsibility as companies scrambled to find living, capable people. The world was a bus dangling from a bridge over an abyss in a high wind. His job was to keep the bus from falling while they figured out how to save it.

The ribbon of the population ticker's endless red numbers reminded him of the children's game, duck, duck, goose. Except it was death, death, death, birth. Too much death. Not nearly enough birth. It felt like a digital hourglass hovering over his head, each death like a grain of sand in his blood, scraping him raw. Unless they reversed the trend, he and his entire generation had only a crumbling, childless future to look forward to.

Of course, who knew for sure if the data was accurate? Entire nations were in chaos, leadership changing like wildfire blowing in the wind. Much of the data was projected based on trends that may or may not still be valid. It could be better than the stats showed. Or, it could be a lot worse.

The world had come back online in fits and starts. Some industries were gone forever. Census taking wasn't on anyone's to-do list at the moment.

Dark things were happening. Everyone was grieving, and some just gave up. The population death rate was increasing despite vast improvements in health care and longevity. Depression was an epidemic, and so was denial.

No one had noticed the existential fire burning beneath all the chaos. Too busy scrambling for immediate survival, the world hadn't realized until several months ago that birth rates had fallen off a cliff. Jared shuddered, thinking about what would happen if they failed.

This was his mission, his burden. It was 7 am, and he'd been in his office for two hours already. It was all about MedPal, a semiplant designed to monitor markers of chronic disease and manipulate the body's natural systems to create and maintain homeostasis.

It had been near launch when the Cyber War broke everything. Eos had recovered the program and added a fertility function. MedPal was created to help ease the healthcare crisis. Now, it was meant to save the world as well. He grunted as he turned back to his desk. Usually, he thrived on pressure.

The cause of the falling birthrate was still unclear, but what was clear was that reproductive hormones were affected. Most men had lowered testosterone, and women had too much androgen. MedPal would regulate hormone levels, and the result would be increased fertility. At least, that was the plan. He had a vested interest. He and his wife had tried to become pregnant for three years before the Crush. Despite the tenuousness of the world, they wanted a child very much.

He called out to the vend stationed by the door. "A matcha latte, please." A decade ago, this would have been a dream office. Office space was plentiful now, and so was technology. People, not so much. He thanked the vend as it glided over to deposit the steaming latte onto his desk.

The results coming in from the beta test were encouraging. Better health outcomes, and most importantly, the test group had a fifteen percent higher pregnancy rate than the control group. It was too soon to be excited. The first trimester was when miscarriages were more likely. Still, it was hopeful.

He finished his drink and moved over to his walking desk. He put the treadmill on high and started a fast jog while he scanned the reports. His muscular legs beneath his casual black pants testified to how much time he spent running while working.

He touched his index and forefinger together to activate his AI assistant. "Sheila set up a team call for as soon as possible."

Her motherly voice replied. "Done. 9:45 am."

"Thanks." He smiled as he remembered how his wife, Emma, had changed the voice of his AI assist from the sultry, smooth female voice he'd chosen to the matronly nanny voice. His colleagues laughed when Sheila reminded him to wear his coat or asked if he was getting enough sleep.

===

"The call is ready," Sheila announced as she activated the wall. Faces from all over the globe appeared.

He stood up, pacing before the screen as he spoke. His slight frame moved with grace and power from a lifetime of martial arts. "We're on T-minus 10. Pre-launch is tomorrow. This is it. Does anyone have anything to tell me before we're a go?" He scrutinized each face as they shook their heads.

"Misha." His eyes bored into the face of the bear-like, unkempt man sitting half a world away. His left eye was twitching; a classic Misha tell.

Misha started, his hand coming to his bushy black beard. "It's nothing. I found a blip. A command sequence that didn't make sense. It was one blip out of trillions of lines of code. It was on the original version and isn't being used on the reboot. Misha shrugged, his eyes avoiding Jared.

"At the risk of sounding cliché, the fate of the entire fucking world rests on MedPal's success, and you didn't think it was something I should know? Everybody else can go. Sheila, remote me into Misha's station. Misha, show me the fucking blip!"

Jared's small frame stilled as he waited for Misha to show him the anomaly. Years of training had taught him to use emotion and stress to clear his mind. His focus was absolute. His fingers moved involuntarily as if they were already working on the problem.

"Misha, how fucking long did this fucking blip last, and how many beta testers were involved?"

"It was recovered from before the reboot. One time, fifty participants, and it was never repeated. We tested it on hundreds of thousands since then. It's statistically insignificant." Misha shrugged again. His accent thickened as it always did when he was tired or stressed. "It is not a problem. AI wrote the code for MedPal. It is likely part of a test they ran on a function that didn't pass the early trials. It is fine."

Jared rubbed his eyes. How was this possible? The MedPal was a semiplant, a device that acted like an implant, worn like a watch with nano interfaces connecting it to the wearer. The nanos could free range in the body, performing maintenance and monitoring myriad bodily functions. It monitored AIC, blood pressure, nutritional levels, and a whole host of other functions. MedPal could tell you what you had for breakfast, the last time you peed, and just about anything else.

They had accelerated the rollout, starting the beta testing three months ago. It had been successful in manipulating reproductive hormones, and that's all that mattered now. He didn't understand the medical part. That wasn't his job. Knowing everything about MedPal *was* his job. He needed to know what this command sequence did.

"Hey, Sheila? Can you see if I can get a quick meeting with Darin?"

"Sure thing," replied Sheila. A moment later, she spoke again. "Darin is available for lunch today. Your schedule is open. Shall I confirm?

"Yes, make it for here in my office and order sushi."

"It's confirmed and on your calendar. Take a deep breath, dearie. You sound stressed." Her lilting, accented voice reminded him of Mrs. Doubtfire from the classic Robin Williams movie.

Jared grunted in reply, engrossed in the work again.

===

"Take a look at this, Darin," said Jared, "I've been reviewing the MedPal test results, and I think there's a command sequence that shouldn't be here."

"Command sequence to do what?" asked Darin, his brow furrowing as he leaned in for a closer look.

"Something it sure as hell shouldn't do. Jared said, highlighting a section of the code. "This shows these subjects had their brain chemistry manipulated, That isn't on any of the protocols."

"It's pre reboot," Darin answered dismissively.

"It's still in the code! I need to know exactly what it does. We damn sure can't have a command sequence triggered that we don't understand."

"I can ask some of the original team members, but a lot of them aren't around. The project was segmented-Chinese walls between divisions to avoid one team knowing too much. Standard protocol at the time to prevent corporate espionage, but a problem for us now."

He continued. "Several of the original teams on the project were decimated. We haven't found anybody from the original data analysis or UX teams; we've only got one person from the original tech architect team. And on the medical side- fuck, we lost them all. R & D died faster than a train jumper. Finding someone who worked on that particular test may be challenging, but I'll try to find something out. There are a lot of pieces missing from this puzzle. We put it back together the best we could with what we had. I'm sure it's nothing. "

"It doesn't appear to be nothing. It looks like MedPal has capabilities that we don't know about."

"I'll do some checking. But don't spend too much time on this. It's history, and we need to move forward. Who knows what they were doing before the world got fucked? "

"Should we delay the launch? "

Darin shook his head. "Nah, the techs and meddies have been all over this since the reboot. I'm sure there's a simple explanation. I'll swing back to you when I have the answer." He gave him a light punch on the shoulder. "Relax, Jared. Maybe you're overdue for some cliff jumping or whatever other crazy shit you do to relax." He turned and walked out of the office.

===

Jared stared at the report, trying to understand what he was seeing. Each new piece of information he uncovered only made the situation more troubling. "Abnormal cortisol levels, heightened aggression, increased impulsivity..." Jared combed through the reports. "This isn't about healing. This is about controlling emotions."

"Sheila, get me Darin again."

Darin was annoyed when he walked back into the office. "Jared, I told you I'd let you know," Darin said, not bothering to hide his irritation. "I checked it, and it's nothing. We've got plenty that needs to be done without chasing ghosts of the past. I told you to let it go."

"Check out these reports." Jared rotated the holograph to face Darin. "This is not medical intervention. It's a manipulation of emotions. It's purposefully fucking with brain chemistry to achieve a specific outcome."

Darin's eyes scanned the holo; his brow furrowed in deep concentration. For a moment, it seemed like he would brush off Jared's concerns again. But when he spoke, his tone had shifted.

"Hey, it's a beautiful day. Let's walk down and get some fresh air." Darin gave the slightest shake of his head as Jared began to speak. He headed toward the door. Jared followed, his confusion evident.

As the glass elevator floated toward the lobby, Jared studied Darin's face, searching for any hint of deception or evasion. He wanted to trust his mentor, who guided him through his career and stood by him during his successes and failures. But Darin wasn't surprised or upset by what he'd seen. Not like he should be.

They rode down in silence, the tension in the elevator rising with their descent. When they got out of the building, Jared turned to Darin. "What the fuck, Darin? Why do I feel like I'm in fucking spy movie right now?"

Darin swore. "I should have known you wouldn't let this go. Listen, this is strictly need-to-know, and if certain people find out that you know, then we are both in a world of shit. Just because the military has been turned into peacekeepers doesn't mean they're all going peacefully. I don't know how treacherous this knowledge is. The world is a big fucking pinata right now, and a lot of different groups are looking to take a swing."

Jared stared at his old friend. "I need to know.", he said.

Darin nodded and began walking towards the park. When they were far from other people, he began to speak. "I didn't find out until it was too late. DOD and a couple of other government agencies you don't even want to know exist had their nasty fingers in this from the start. They were looking at military uses, manipulating soldiers' hormones so that they create more aggressive soldiers. You saw the shit they did during the Cyber War. Cutting power to hospitals and attacking civilian populations in ways that were unthinkable." He started walking faster, his agitation clear in his stride.

"I thought it was just pre-war shit, but some of the data has been accessed since we rebooted. Whoever accessed it covered their tracks. I can't find anything else out, but I'm keeping an eye on it. You have to let me handle it."

He smiled, but it was forced. "I guess some old military people are still looking to be relevant. Let it be, Jared."

Jared barked out a harsh laugh. "Yeah, sure, and we trust the military? Shit, Darin, you don't believe that crap? You expect me to look away when this could endanger everything?"

Darin shrugged. "You know the military will never believe in peace. The world changed on a dime. Some institutions crumble slowly, but they do crumble. Don't do anything stupid, buddy. It'll be all right. The tests showed problems they couldn't fix. Soldiers turning on each other, aggression towards officers, uncontrollable behavior, They tanked it. It's history. I can't protect you if you keep poking at this."

Jared clenched his fists. He began the slow, focused breathing he'd learned in martial arts as a child to calm himself down so he could process the information Darin had revealed. As much as he trusted Darin, he didn't trust whoever might be accessing MedPal without his knowledge.

"All right," Jared said, knowing he could only push so far, "but what about the civilian applications? The 200,000 beta testers who are already using MedPal? The millions who will be getting devices over the next few weeks? We need to remove that command sequence, Darin."

Darin sighed, rubbing the back of his neck. "You know as well as I do, we're too far along to start fucking with the code now. Hell, we still don't understand some of it yet. We have to move forward. The consumer applications are safe."

"Safe?" Jared's voice rose with incredulity. "We're talking about fucking manipulating people's brain chemistry here! The Musky Principle will surely apply here. *If evil can be done with technology, evil men will seek that technology*. Don't forget about the man who inspired that principle. He's still one of the richest men on the planet and spends his money trying to design the world to fit his belief of how things should be, regardless of the cost to other humans. The world has too many others like him-men and women who will stop at nothing to gain power and control. There's nothing safe about this, Darin."

"Jared, I know how it sounds. But trust me, we're doing everything we can to ensure the safety and well-being of our users. We've got teams working around the clock to monitor and adjust as needed. The surgeon general's office and the FDA, or what's left of it, are overseeing this. It's okay. It was a one-time thing. It was pre-reboot, You need to drop it."

Jared stared at his mentor, torn between trusting him and wanting to dig deeper into the issue. Humanity would end without MedPal's ability to increase fertility, and there was no plan B. Better to have a flawed solution than no solution. He didn't really have a choice at this point.

"Fine," he said through gritted teeth, "but I will keep my eyes open. And if I find anything remotely suspicious, I'm coming back to you."

"Fair enough," Darin conceded, nodding. "It's a clusterfuck, but we're in a lesser of two evils situation here. We found out too late, and despite the Accords, people are still trying to keep things like they were."

===

Determined to understand what else MedPal might be capable of, Jared spent the next two days poring over MedPal's test data and cross-referencing it with other research studies.

"Work, dammit, work," Jared said, staring at the holo, willing the code he'd just put finished to work. The tenacity that had driven him to be a champion black belt in both Aikido and Kung Fu made him relentless when he had a goal in mind. He was going to put in his own safeguards.

The world had suffered enough from putting trust in systems that weren't as strong or resilient as they should have been. Tech had taken exponential leaps forward as AI progressed, and even the people who thought they understood it were caught off guard by its capabilities. Jared had no intention of being one of them.

"Take that!" he whispered triumphantly as the alert he'd put in the code pinged back at him. He wasn't naive enough to believe someone wouldn't someday try to deploy the technology. The Musky principle always held true. The Cyber War had proved that beyond a shadow of a doubt.

If the command sequence was triggered, he would get an alert and could decide on what to do. In the meantime, he would keep watch.

Jared leaned back in his chair, satisfied and apprehensive. He had no idea what he would or even could do if the alert was triggered. He needed to have an answer before that happened. If there was one thing that you could count on, it was whoever was fucking around with the MedPal; they weren't going to stop.

Chapter 2: Mapenzie

Mapenzie opened her eyes as the blinds rose to let in the early sunlight. The windows opened, and the sea breeze drifted through the room. She smiled as the sound of the ocean filled the room. The salty taste of the air always brought her a sense of clarity.

She stretched her long limbs beneath the silk sheets, her lithe body emerging as she sat in bed. Her long box braids fell over her shoulders as she swung her legs over the edge of the mattress and padded barefoot toward the bathroom.

Her reflection in the full-length mirror caught her eye – tall, athletic, and exuding confidence. She admired her perfect ebony skin as the lights turned on as she entered the bathroom.

"Shower." She said as she dropped her robe and stepped into the gleaming glass cage. The water flowed over her at the precise temperature she preferred. She stood while the jets and flexiarms massaged, soaped, rinsed, and dried her. She stretched languidly to give the flexiarms access.

"Moisturize." A fine mist of her signature blend of oils floated over her, and a gentle, warm breeze blew over her while the flexiarms rubbed the oil in. She stood for a few extra minutes, enjoying the feel of the fingers as they kneaded her stiff muscles.

A sexy smile flitted over her face as she thought of the other attachments in her shower. Despite being between lovers, she still had a full and satisfying sex life. She wasn't one of those who wanted a sexbot, but there was nothing wrong with some help to relax her at the end of the day. Nikki Minaj's *Pink Lady Girls* flitted through her mind.

As she walked into the kitchen, a ping announced a call. She double-clicked her fingers, and her mother's hologram sprang to life. "Good morning, sugar," her mother said. "How you feelin' today?"

"Morning, Mama," Mapenzie replied, watching as the automated kitchen finished preparing her morning smoothie. She got a real kick from watching the refrigerator dispense the fruit into the blender. "I'm doing great. Excited for the prelaunch of MedPal today."

"Oh, the MedPal thingie," her mother hesitated, concern creasing her forehead, "I'm a little scared. You know I don't like things poking around in my body."

"Mama, trust me. It will be so good for you," Mapenzie reassured her, picking up her morning smoothie. "You won't notice a thing. You put it on your wrist, and it does the rest. You'll have instant access to medical advice, and it'll monitor your health in real-time. You won't have to remember to take your medication. It does it for you. I've done my research. The company is legit, and their technology is top-notch."

Her mother nodded. "I trust you, sugar pie. You've always understood this newfangled tech stuff. It just makes my head spin. This AI stuff scares me. I've heard so much about it."

"It's not generative AI, Mama. That's all strictly controlled by the Accords. The AI functions are limited to what will help you stay healthy. I won't have to worry so much about you. I know you get lonely since Daddy died."

"Seems like half the world died."

"I know, Mama. But we're here, and always taught me to look at what I got and not what I don't. I love you. I gotta run."

Mapenzie finished her smoothie as the hologram faded away. She wondered if she wasn't becoming spoiled by all the tech. What the hell was even in the smoothie she was drinking? She didn't remember.

She clicked her fingers to turn on one of the wall screens. She scrolled through, stopping briefly on a preview for a new vid. The promo showed Beyonce' whispering, "You can't handle the truth," to her on-screen lover, a young Sidney Poiter. Like all vids today, Mapenzie could star in her own version by uploading a short video of herself, and AI would replace Beyonce' with her. She clicked off. Time to get to work.

She hummed Michael Jackson's *Man in the Mirror* as she got ready to do her daily vid. She pursed her lips to give her flawless image an air kiss before snapping her fingers to activate the recording. Almost everything was different now, but social media was pretty much the same. It was more predominant now that traditional media was extinct. People got their news from influencers they trusted. She'd heard a rumor that an AI vid scrubber was in the works. It would give a truth score to vids. That would be good for her.

"But what is truth? Is truth unchanging law? We both have truths. Are mine the same as yours? Mapenzie sang to herself as she fiddled with the lighting for her video. It was a song from an old musical her mother loved. Mapenzie's mind always had a playlist for whatever she was thinking.

Journalists were front-line soldiers in the information war, and their casualty rate was high. The truth was what you wanted it to be. A few of the prewar journalists were still on YouTube. The rest were collateral damage. If they were still alive, they had no industry to return to.

Social media was the wild, wild west, and Mapenzie knew how to ride that horse. The content you could access these days was crazy. Some guy from pre-Crush was still raving like a rabid dog about things he knew nothing about, but he was sure everybody who didn't look or think like him was to blame.

The sexbot industry loved him and his followers. They were money in the bank for an industry built on creating fake relationships for people who weren't capable of real ones. He was one of the many people trying to live in a world so far gone it was dust and memories. Fuckin' boomers.

A guy out of Florida- Terry Spencer- probably a made-up name- had tens of millions of followers on YouTube. He was an AP reporter who'd retired several years before the Crush but had come out of retirement when so many of his colleagues had fallen. Something about him evoked the simpler times when decent people lived ordinary lives, rising to become extraordinary in answer to the needs of the time. He was the king of Dad jokes, and everybody needed a laugh these days. Corny as hell, but it worked. He and Tyler Perry's Madea were the current King and Queen of social media. They were both bussin'.

The media landscape had changed overnight. SNL's final real show was the most-watched one in history, still being viewed millions of times yearly. AI was still creating SNL, but it wasn't the same. It turns out that crazy funny is unpredictable, and no matter how smart you are or how much history you can access, you can't replicate creative chaos. There are things that make us human that cannot be dissected, analyzed, or reproduced by any measure of intelligence.

Social media was the new gold rush, and people rose to fame and were knocked back down like moles in the old Whack-a-mole game. It was from this chaos that Mapenzie had made a name for herself. She was rational. She was attractive. She wasn't afraid to have an opinion. She was lucky. So far.

She'd been a minor influencer before the world crumbled and managed to continue through most of the chaos. Her calm, optimistic videos gave people hope through the dark times. Her earlier videos were streams of consciousness filled with words of comfort and faith. She shared tips for foraging for food and staying warm, making people feel like better days would come. Even when people had just a few minutes of phone charge from a solar charger or a generator, if it were a day when the internet or the phone service was working, they'd check in with Mapenzie.

When the better days she had promised had come, she pivoted to AI reviews. She was one of the first to embrace AI innovations before the Crush and became the person to watch if you needed to understand anything about AI. Her consistency during that long, dark winter had helped people to feel like they weren't alone. She kept telling them that the world wasn't ending. It was the birth of a new world.

When the new world she had promised was birthed, she reminded them that she had kept her promise. She brought them hope, showing them the way to a better world. She had millions of followers and was one of the longest-running successful influencers left standing. She took nothing for granted. Every video was planned, and every gesture and word was rehearsed.

===

Her vibrant personality filled the screen. "Hey, everyone. Mapenzie here. Today is the big day," she announced. We're here to become part of the brave new world of healthcare for all! The MedPal semiplant is pre-launching, and trust me when I say this device will change your life. Imagine having instant access to medical advice, personalized health monitoring, and more, all just a thought away. MedPlant is the future of healthcare, and it's here now! "

She smiled as she finished and pointed her index finger to the floor. "You know what to do! There is a link below to preorder the device. Please subscribe, like, and share! Let's create a happier, healthier world for everyone, together!"

Her followers' comments flooded in, expressing their amazement and eagerness to get their hands on the revolutionary device. Mapenzie expertly engaged with them, answering questions and addressing concerns with charm and confidence.

"Y'all know I love my Mama, but she lives a few hours away. MedPal for us means I have real-time access to her health data and will be alerted when anything goes out of balance. It's a real comfort for both of us and will make the distance seem less. It's like having a doctor on your wrist."

She finished up the livestream and headed out for her morning swim.

===

Mapenzie glided through the water, her thoughts wandering. Her followers trusted her opinions and recommendations, but a nagging thought began to surface in the back of her mind: What if something went wrong? Her entire life- and considerable income- was wrapped up in the MedPal launch.

She'd been instrumental in AI launches before, but MedPal was more than a companion or a house bot. If something went wrong, she was the face of MedPal for millions of people. The refrain from the truth song kept running through her head, speeding up. *"Crucify him! Crucify him! Crucifyhimrucifyhimcrucifyhim!"* She remembered Pilate's response to the song. *"But to keep you vultures happy, I shall flog him."*

A cool breeze whispered over her body as she exited the pool, water streaming onto the deck. That wasn't the only reason she shivered. The words of the truth song still echoed in the back of her mind, but not so much that she couldn't concentrate. She shook them off as she dressed for lunch with some friends. "I'm just picking up Mama's vibes from this morning. People have freaked out at every tech innovation in human history, convinced that it would end the world."

Hearing her voice make the declaration brought her peace. She'd done her homework. It was a significant advancement for billions of people with access to better health care. It would solve the fertility crisis. It was fine. She was fine. Even if it all disappeared tomorrow, Mapenzie had plenty of money stashed in many places.

After lunch, she sat down to check her channel. "Twenty-seven million views! Wow, even for me, that's a lot, " she thought as she read through the comments her AI Assist had curated for her.

"Mapenzie, I respect your opinion on the MedPal device, but do you think we're losing something important here? The human touch in healthcare is crucial, and I'm afraid these AI devices will only drive us further apart." - BotFan Jo

She addressed the issue during a live video, hoping to spark an honest conversation with her followers. "Let's talk about your questions," Mapenzie began, her tone more serious than before. "One of my amazing followers raised concerns about the MedPal device and the potential loss of human connection in healthcare. Help me answer BotFan Jo. What do you all think? Do you share this concern, or do you believe AI can enhance our lives without sacrificing our humanity?"

The comments poured in once again, sparking a lively debate among her followers. Some staunchly defended AI technology, while others echoed the same fears that Mapenzie was grappling with.

"This was a great talk, peeps. You know I love hearing what you think. For me, I'm 98% pro-AI. If you remember your history, we've always had fears around tech and figured it out, and the world was made better. That's what I believe, and I have the lifestyle to prove it. Perhaps one morning, I'll do a live from my shower and let you all see how much fun it can be." With a sexy smile and a slow wink, she signed off.

"No matter how advanced we might be, the old adage. 'Nothing sells like sex' still applies." She thought as she pondered how she could do a PG-13 version of a live from her shower.

===

"Over here, Mapenzie." Her friend Keara had already gotten them a table. Restaurants were one of the things that weren't all the way back, so getting in was sometimes hard. There was always a table for Mapenzie, though.

Mapenzie walked over and sang out, "*I do my hair toss.*" She did an exaggerated hair toss. Keara stood up and sang, "*Check my nails.*" They both sang "*Feelin' good as hell!*" and then hugged. Laughing, they sat down. It was a ritual they'd done since high school.

"Girl, your livestream today was on fire! I've never seen so many people loving on you," Kiara enthused, sipping her blue cocktail.

"Yeah, it's getting a little intense. Hope I'm not flying too high."

"What do you mean?"

"I got my whole gig in MedPal. What if something crazy happens? If anything goes wrong, the shit will roll right down to me. Sometimes I wonder if we aren't going overboard on this AI shit again. I was thinking today about how totally tech-dependent I am. I'm not sure it's all good."

"Mapenzie, you say it all the time. We live in the world we have, not the one we want. I know you, girl, and I know you did your homework."

"Damn straight, I did my homework. But sometimes I feel like I spend more time with AI than I do people anymore. Maybe I should find something else to do."

"Meanwhile, you've got a damn good gig going. You could have all the people you want. AI's just easier sometimes. Why have some man candy sitting on your couch messing things up, then snoring in your bed when you can take care of your own damn self in the shower and then cuddle up with a good vid?"

Mapenzie forced a smile, but her thoughts remained troubled as they continued to chat through the evening.

===

The following day, her wall screen vibrated incessantly, notifications flooding in from her social media accounts. "Read me my top comments," She instructed her AI Assist. As she listened, she found herself at the center of a negative backlash from followers who had discovered her conversation with Keara.

"Can't believe @MapenzieGrailer is complaining about her life! Some people are never satisfied," one follower wrote, while another added, "Guess AI isn't perfect, huh, Mapenzie? Maybe you should rethink your whole brand."

Her heart raced as she listened to the comments, realizing that her moment of vulnerability had now become a source of public scrutiny. Probably, a nearby table or one of the servers had recognized her. It was a lesson learned. She was a public figure now and needed to be on her game every time she stepped out of the house. The refrain echoed again. "*Crucify him*!" Except in her head, they were singing, "*Crucify her*!"

She cursed out loud and picked up a book from the table. It hit the wall with a satisfying thunk. She would have to answer this with confidence. Evolution always had winners and losers. When car travel overtook horse travel, the stables, groomers, and feed providers didn't die; they reinvented themselves. The same would happen with AI, wouldn't it? And no matter what, Mapenzie was going to be a winner.

"Seraphina, record," she instructed the AI." Mapenzie gathered her thoughts and began speaking. She would answer this, and her followers would understand. They loved her, didn't they?

Chapter 3: Hali

Sunlight streamed through the window, casting a warm glow over the small but well-equipped clinic. The sterile room was softened by gentle lighting and warm yellow paint on the walls. Cheerful, soothing music filled the air, and the clinic smelled of lavender. The traditional sterile exam tables had been replaced with friendly-looking chairs that could move into any position with just a gentle word.

Hali Bergero, the clinic director, stood by the window, her silhouette framed by the light. Her shoulders curved inward, resulting from years hunched over screens and patients. Her green eyes exuded warmth, reflecting the empathy that had driven her to pursue medicine in the first place. Her soft brown hair was pulled back into a no-nonsense bun at the nape of her neck, but a few tendrils escaped to frame her intelligent face. She was in her early forties, but her face was lined and creased beyond her years. Like many who had suffered through the past few years, she had lived lifetimes in a very short time.

The Crush had almost broken her. But a good friend had helped her. Jenna was a therapist and had shared something her great-grandmother, a holocaust survivor, had written in a journal.

"Hard times came for us, and people did horrible things. All we could do was hold our hearts steady and as open as we could to the others with us. Death slept beside us, and we had to make friends with it. When it was over, I let it shape rather than scar me. I let it make my hard edges softer so that I was more resilient and pliant to the world. I remind myself every day that I am not what was done to me. I remind myself that holding onto the horrors that I saw only keeps the people who were brutalized trapped in that brutality in my memory. To set them free, and to set myself free, I have to hold the memories of the love before the atrocity-to see those I lost in the wholeness and happiness that they were before it all happened. That is how I choose to remember them. That is how I choose to be shaped." Hali had copied that page and kept it on her desk.

She read it over and over again when the memories of all the deaths she'd seen and the helplessness she'd felt loomed over her like a tsunami waiting to sweep her away.

She was lucky to be part of the MedPal beta test. This meant Hali could care for more patients and have time to listen to their needs. She whispered a prayer of thanks as she readied herself to start her day.

===

"Morning, Dr. Bergero!" A cheerful voice called out as she entered an exam room, accompanied by a snaggle-toothed grin.

"Good morning, Mr. Thompson!" Hali smiled. "How is your MedPal treating you today?"

"Excellent! " He responded. "I never thought I'd be able to track my blood pressure so easily, and the tailored exercise recommendations have made me feel ten years younger!" He ran his hand over his shiny bald head. "Now you just have to program it to grow my hair back!" His guffaw filled the room.

Hali's eyes sparkled with pleasure as she listened to her patient. "I'm glad being part of the beta testing is good for you! Just remember not to push yourself too hard, all right?

"Of course, doc," Mr. Thompson assured her with a playful smirk. "I'm not planning to run any marathons anytime soon."

"Great!" Hali chuckled. "Ready for the next phase? Soon enough, you won't need me at all."

As the two exchanged banter, Hali couldn't help but marvel at how MedPal had transformed her practice. Before its advent, physicians like herself were swamped by a never-ending stream of administrative tasks and insurance companies that controlled everything from the amount of time they could spend with patients to what they could charge for their services.

Now, the AI-driven system took care of all the data collection and analysis, allowing her to focus on what truly mattered – her patients. She'd been a part of the beta test for six months, and the upcoming rollout was exciting. Of course, she was an exception right now, but as MedPal took the pressure off the healthcare system, more doctors could practice as she did, and the patients would have better outcomes and more timely care. People needed people, and not just because that old song said so.

"By the way, Dr. Bergero," Mr. Thompson added while Hali examined the data from his MedPal. "I've been following the dietary plan suggested by MedPal, and I've already lost five pounds! It gives me recipes and everything!"

"That's just wonderful!" Hali exclaimed, letting him see how proud she was of his progress. "Keep it up, Mr. Thompson! You're doing great." It was so nice to have good news.

"All right! You're all set," Hali announced, satisfied with the checkup. "Keep following MedPal's advice, and I'll see you in a few months for your next appointment."

"Will do, doc," he agreed, extending a hand for a firm shake. "Thanks again for everything."

"Of course," Hali responded as she bid him farewell.

===

Hali's screen buzzed. Glancing at it, she saw a text message from her sister Sarah: "Hey, sis, I'm in the waiting room."

"Sarah?" Hali called out as she opened the door to find her sister lounging on the waiting room couch, her black combat boots propped up on the coffee table. She was taller than Hali; her blond hair was shaved on one side and colored a vibrant orange on the other. Very few people would guess that they were sisters.

"Ah, there you are!" Sarah greeted her with a hug and a mischievous smile. "I thought I'd drop by and surprise you. And I brought you something." She pulled a small package from her bag and tossed it to Hali.

"Twinkies?" Hali asked, catching the contraband snack cakes. "How do you find these things? These are illegal, Sarah!"

"C'mon, Sis- You'd give your left arm for some Godiva, and you know it!"

"Ha! You know I wouldn't. Pinkie toe, maybe." She reached over and touched a strand of Sarah's hair. Orange this week, huh? I think I miss the bright blue."

Sarah grinned. "You'll bail me out if the Twinkie police get me, won't ya, sis? We all need a little sweetness." She said, pulling a strand of her hair forward and looking at it. "I'm thinking forest green next."

Hali rolled her eyes and smiled. "You'll never change." Sarah resisted modernity at every turn – at least parts of it. Her irreverence was infectious, but she seemed to be trying to keep parts of the past alive. Parts Hali thought should go.

Hali was more like a parent than a sister to Sarah. Sarah was a surprise, a menopause baby that had arrived when Hali was 17. Her parents' sudden demise in a car crash six years later almost derailed Hali's medical career. Fortunately, their Aunt Jane had stepped up. Her mother's younger sister had been a big part of their lives, so having her help raise Hali was a godsend. Sometimes, Hali thought they were still raising her. At 26, she sometimes behaved like a recalcitrant teenager.

Aunt Jane was also resistant to the changes that AI was bringing. Hali loved and respected her aunt, but the relationship was somewhat strained since Jane had moved back to her home outside of the city. It was only an hour by AutoAuto, but Hali hadn't visited much recently. She wasn't sure why. It seemed like she was a thousand years older than her aunt. Hali had been on the front lines of the Crush and the Cyber War. The idea of happiness and peace wavered like a mirage in her mind. She feared that if she reached for them, they would disappear.

"Come on, live a little," Sarah urged, poking Hali in the side. "You spend all day helping people follow the rules. Loosen up! Break a few rules. It won't be the end of the world. That already happened." She winked at Hali and guffawed at her own joke.

"You can poison yourself if you choose. " Hali grumbled, handing back the Twinkie package. A smile lurked in her eyes. "But don't expect me to administer your insulin when you develop diabetes. These things are illegal for a reason."

"Sure thing, Sis," Sarah responded, raising her hand in a mock salute before biting into her Twinkie. She wiped the white cream from the corner of her mouth and gave an exaggerated moan of pleasure. "MMMMMMM..chemicals. So yummy!"

"Ugh, you're insufferable," Hali said, shaking her head. Arguing with Sarah was an exercise in futility, but she couldn't help but worry about her sister's disdain for authority and the strain it put on their relationship. They were such opposites. Hali worried about everything, and Sarah never had a care.

"I am," Sarah admitted through a mouthful of Twinkie, "but at least I'm keeping things interesting!"

Hali pursed her lips and glanced at her MedPal notification, which informed her that her next patient, Emma, had just arrived for her appointment. She gave Sarah a pointed stare.

"All right, all right," Sarah conceded, stuffing the remainder of the Twinkie into her bag. "I'll leave you to your patients. Just remember what I said – sometimes breaking the rules is good. You need to loosen up! And Aunt Jane says she missed you and wants you to visit."

"Tell her I will," Hali replied, ushering Sarah towards the door. "And tell her I love her. Give her a hug for me." She hugged Sarah goodbye, feeling a little guilty. She'd been working nonstop since she'd been included in the MedPal pretrials. Being part of the beta test was heady stuff. And it kept her from her memories. Still, she needed to spend time with her family. She returned to her desk and told herself that she would visit soon.

===

Reading the latest MedPal updates, Hali marveled at how much her profession had changed in the past few years. The dark, soul-crushing days of the pandemic and Cyber War had almost ended her. They had to choose who to connect to the few generator-fueled ventilators and who to let die. Working seven days a week, grabbing food and sleep wherever they could- it had taken a toll on everyone in the medical profession.

She was unable to do anything but comfort people as they died from injuries and diseases she should have been able to save them from Sometimes she couldn't even offer comfort as she rushed to the next bedside.

It had taken an enormous toll. She still woke up in the middle of the night and found herself on her feet, rushing to the next patient, her hands reaching for the stethoscope that had lived around her neck for a year before she realized she was home in her room. Usually, she would stand there and cry. Other times, she'd try to go back to bed, but the faces of the dead and dying marched through her mind, and she found herself counting the dead instead of sheep.

At the worst of it, they had been thrown back in time to what medicine had been before electricity and modern pharmaceuticals. In the first few days after the breakdown of power and transportation, they ran out of everything. There were no supply chains and no deliveries of life-saving drugs. The generators worked for a while, but they ran out of gas, plunging them further into the dark and despair that marked that time. The people who had stayed at their posts, from firefighters to police to delivery drivers and warehouse workers, had accomplished Herculean tasks, but even Hercules could be broken.

Surgeries stopped except for a few desperate attempts. Burst appendixes would kill either way— internal blockages or infected limbs- where the choice was to try or die. The survival rates were abysmal. Eventually, they stopped trying, and there was no morphine to help people to die humanely. There were rumors of nurses suffocating the suffering with pillows to keep them from screaming out their agony in the last hours or days of their lives. Nobody wanted to talk about it. Nobody wanted to know. If it happened, it was horrible. If it didn't happen, it was horrible. What good would come of knowing? Hali had seen it in the faces of the others in her support group. People destined to live with the desperate choices they never asked for but couldn't avoid. They were all haunted by the same ghosts.

Despite the Sisyphean nature of the work, a remarkable number of her colleagues stayed at their posts and did what they could. Everyone had PTSD. Hell, the world had PTSD. It wasn't uncommon to find people sobbing on the street or gasping for air from a panic attack. Anything could set it off—a person wearing the same coat as a dead loved one. A glance in the window shows an unrecognizable face, gaunt with suffering and loss, and then you realize it is your reflection. Even a sunny day could trigger a memory that would bring you to your knees.

Things were better now, but the world was still in crisis. It was a slow-motion crisis, and for people who had been fighting for their very survival a short time ago, it was easy to pretend it wasn't happening. Too many expected it would end like the disaster movies of old. Undoubtedly, the unlikely heroes would band together and save the world.

Even after the devastation they'd endured, people still believed someone would save them. For the couples trying to have children, the desperate ticking of biological clocks drowned out fragile hope. They worried themselves into a death spiral, the stress of potential failure increasing the likelihood of permanent failure.

She was grateful that Sarah and Aunt Jane had been safe in the countryside, but it had been a dark and lonely time, and her scars were deep and many. She had seen too many colleagues succumb to the miasma of despair that haunted them all. She was trained for the blood, guts, and offal she had swum in during that time-operating like an automaton as she moved from one patient to the next. It had almost broken her. Aunt Jane's tender heart would have been ripped to pieces had she been in the city among all the constant, gritty horrors.

Fewer people had died out where Sarah and Jane lived. The community had mourned together, and it brought them even closer. They weren't in an endless loop of watching strangers die alone, unmourned, because trying to notify next of kin was impossible.

Hali forced herself back to the present. So much had changed so rapidly. Most of it was good, it seemed. Time will tell.

Banning the stew of chemicals that had become the mainstay of processed foods had caused a massive disruption in the food supply, but it had gotten better now. Farm-fresh, regeneratively grown food was readily available, and a whole generation had been forced to learn how to cook. Having fewer people to feed also helped the food shortages.

Many people believed that the chronic ill health of the general population had allowed the many variants to run rampant through the population, and processed foods were blamed.

The world normalized the overprocessed, nutritionless food system, even as obesity and disease ripped the joys of childhood from the children. How strange that it all appears so clear in retrospect when the evidence was there all along, and many people had been shouting about the dangers. Complacency is its own disease, she supposed.

AutoAg meant anyone could grow food, and parking lots and abandoned factories had become farms. Populations were getting healthier from the food, but a lot of processed food was still in basements and back alleys all over the world. Sarah frequented the black markets, where M&M's and Twinkies were the new contraband. It was dangerous, and Hali worried about the escapades of her little sister.

The ping announcing her next patient was ready brought Hali out of her reverie. There was no point in living in the past. The future was hopeful.

===

"Hi, Emma," Hali greeted her, gesturing for her to take a seat. "It's good to see you again. What can I do for you today?" Only about half of Hali's patients were in the MedPal beta test, and she enjoyed the old routine of a physical exam. Emma was one of her non-beta patients.

"Hi, Dr. Bergero," Emma mumbled, slumping on the exam chair. "I've just been... I don't know; I've been down."

Emma was petite and graceful, her delicate features framed by a cascade of chestnut curls. Her typically expressive blue eyes seemed dull.

"Tell me what's been going on," Hali said as she began the physical exam of her patient. "Have there been any particular events or changes in your life?"

Emma hesitated momentarily, her eyes darting around the room before settling on her hands in her lap. "It's just... everything feels so overwhelming sometimes," she began, her voice just above a whisper. "Ever since AI took over most of my bookkeeping business, I've had more time for my hobbies and charity work, which is great. But sometimes, I can't help but feel... useless. And, of course, like everyone else, we can't get pregnant. What if this is my life? Just crocheting blankets and crying for days every time I get my period?"

"Emma, you're not useless," Hali said. "And MedPal might be able to help you conceive. You're doing important work with the reeducation project and making a difference in people's lives."

"I know," Emma sighed, her shoulders slumping. "But sometimes it's hard to remember that when everything else seems so... automated. Even volunteering isn't like before. So many people have nothing to do and want to volunteer. It's hard to get a time slot."

"Everyone is struggling with the changes," Hali said. "And feeling overwhelmed or even a little lost amid such rapid changes is normal. I want you to remember that you're not alone in this. A lot of people are feeling like you are, and there are support groups and clubs you can attend. Let me sign you up for the MedPal prelaunch so we can get more information about what is happening inside your body."

"Thank you, Dr. Bergero," Emma whispered, her eyes glistening with unshed tears. "I appreciate you. It means a lot."

"Take care, Emma. I'll see you again soon," Hali said as she opened the door.

Chapter 4: Whispers

As Hali was getting ready to leave for the day, another message came from Sarah. She was in the waiting room. Hali could see her pacing the room as she walked toward her.

"You're wearing out my carpet, Sarah. What's wrong, sweetie?" Hali watched her sister's uncharacteristic nervousness, concern flickering in her bright green eyes. Sarah stopped and turned to Hali, her playful demeanor gone.

"Have you seen Mapenzie's latest video? The comments from followers are full of crazy theories about what will happen when MedPal devices are on everyone's wrist. People think it's about mind control, slavery- all sorts of diabolical plots."

Hali raised an eyebrow, skepticism tugging at her lips. "You know how I feel about conspiracy theories, Sarah. Just sad, scared people who don't like change." Her gaze softened as she saw distress on her sister's face. "Why are you so worried?"

"I'm afraid there's going to be violence around the launch, and as one of the first physicians to embrace it, I'm worried about you. Please be careful. Read the comments on Mapenzie's feed and at least know what people are saying. Just in case it gets ugly."

===

Hali sighed, then pulled up Mapenzie's social media page and clicked on the latest video. The influencer appeared on screen, her voice steady and her gaze intense. Hali tried to keep an open mind but couldn't shake the feeling that Mapenzie was just another "influencer" who would peddle anything to make a buck.

"All this controversy must be great for Mapenzie. Lots of views and comments mean more money for her, right?"

"She's not like that, sis. I've known her since grade school. She wouldn't promote something she didn't believe in. Her favorite aunt died from a stroke because of undiagnosed hypertension. She's trying hard to overcome the conspiracies and talk sense into people. Would you be willing to meet with her and give her some data so she can answer these crazies? I'll feel better if there isn't so much controversy, and she's got the ear of a lot of people."

"Okay, "I'll meet with Mapenzie and see what data I can give her. I'm all about the data." Hali looked at her sister. "It's not like you to be so serious about anything. Is anything else going on? Anything you want to talk about?"

Sarah just shrugged. Her smile seemed forced. "Someday, I might want to live in a different world. Sooner or later, the world will run out of Twinkies, and then where will I be?" She wiped her brow dramatically, a genuine smile finally coming out. Hali couldn't help but smile back.

On the screen, Mapenzie continued. "I hear you, "she said, sincerity coming from her in waves, like sunbeams coming through the clouds. "These conspiracy theories are baseless rumors. MedPal will save lives and give us back the ability to have children."

Her charisma was undeniable, and Hali couldn't help but be drawn in by her magnetic presence. Mapenzie finished up. "People have feared change since the beginning of time. We've been through a lot these past few years, but a new day is here. Embrace it!"

"It's probably not a bad idea to get out ahead of the rumors. Are you going to join us?"

"Depends on when you meet. I've got a line on some Hostess Ding Dongs I'm trying to chase down." With that, she was out the door.

===

Jared sat at the kitchen table with his wife, Emma, a steaming cup of homemade tea in front of him. It was Emma's favorite room in the house. She loved the tiled backdrop with accent tiles of herbs and flowers. The gleaming counters held spice racks and jars of dried herbs she'd grown herself. Copper-bottomed pots hung on the wall, and a bowl of fresh fruit sat on the table.

Glass jars lined one countertop, filled with different types of flour and sugar. Emma loved experimenting with baking. Her new favorite cake was a combination of breadfruit and cassava flour mixed with just a bit of almond flour. She hadn't baked in a while, not since the depression started. She imagined the jars staring at her forlornly, wondering why she had abandoned them.

A hanging basket with mint cascading down filled one corner. On the windowsill, a long planter overflowing with different herbs vying for attention and not getting any.

Looking out the window, Emma could see the AutoAg maintaining the garden beds full of fresh, organic vegetables and flowers. It used to make her happy. Now, she just felt numb. She could see the colors, but they all had a gray, dull haze. Nothing mattered. It was all just too much effort. The bright, piney notes of rosemary filled the air as they discussed Emma's recent battle with depression.

"Jared, I've been struggling even more lately," Emma said. "Dr. Bergero mentioned that the MedPal might be a good treatment option for me."

Jared froze, his mind racing. Of course, he should have realized that this would happen. He'd been so wrapped up that he forgot that Emma's doctor was part of the beta test. Shit, shit, shit! What should he do? After what he'd learned, there was no way he would let her get the device. She would want to ask questions he wasn't prepared to answer. He didn't want to share his concerns. She was under enough stress. None of his inner turmoil showed as he replied, "I don't think that's the best option right now, Em."

"What?! I don't understand. MedPal is your baby. You've lived and breathed it for months, telling me how it will help so many people. Now you don't want it to help me? How else are we going to get pregnant!?"

"Emma, I..." Jared began, then paused, struggling to find the right words. He didn't want to burden her with his knowledge, but neither could he endorse a treatment after he'd learned what the device was capable of.

"We should explore other options first. Let's wait a while. They've beta-tested on over 200,000 subjects, but I've been in tech a long time. Please wait a few months until a wider range of people have used it. Beta testing gets most of the bugs, but first trials uncover things, too. Better to wait."

"Jared, I'm not buying it," Emma said, disbelief on her face. "You're the AI guy. What's happening?"

"Let's go to the doctor together and explore other options first." He let go of the breath he was holding as she nodded.

Chapter 5: Delusion

Hali waited impatiently for Mapenzie to answer the call. Sarah didn't ask her for help often. She would always be there for her little sister. She still wasn't 100% convinced that the influencer wasn't just about money, but she would meet with her for Sarah's sake.

"I'm here," Mapenzie said as she finally came on. "Thanks for calling. Sarah takes these comments seriously for some reason. What do you think?"

"I think Sarah hangs out with some people who might know things we don't, so it's worth listening to. People convinced they're being lied to can be dangerous."

"True. Can you come to see me? I've learned my lesson about conversations in public. I can send a car. "

"No need; I've got a subscription I rarely ever use. I still get a kick from riding in a Tesla with no driver."

===

Hali admired the Spanish Colonial façade as the Tesla slid through the massive gates. The property was hidden from the street by dense foliage, including fruit trees heavy with fruit and exotic vines that perfumed the air. Hali glanced around as the robot butler led her to the lanai. "Nice digs! I should rethink my career choices." She greeted Mapenzie.

"Public life isn't as glamorous as people think. I do enjoy my toys, however. Did you notice my butlerbot sounds like Chadwick Boseman? I like to close my eyes and pretend he's still alive. They make a humanoid version of him. It freaks me out a bit."

"I haven't kept up with the humanoids. Some doctors are using them as assistants. I still prefer human humans, but the humanoids are damn convincing." Hali answered.

"'Noids are so believable because the sex industry poured billions into sexbots. We'd still have the R2D2 models if it weren't for them. I wonder if all the zombie movies of the nineties weren't some sort of collective presaging for the humanoid replicas. I've heard of some people buying customized versions of dead loved ones. That's creepy, right?"

"We need people having relationships with other real people if we're going to solve our fertility crisis. Mental illnesses are a huge issue now, too. Helping people stay in their delusions can't end well."

"I think AI saved us from ourselves once and will do it again. Without the Accords, we'd still be dying. There's always a dark side, but the collective good being done outweighs the bad, I think."

"I hope you're right."

They settled in on the lanai, an arrangement of refreshments in front of them. The ocean breeze was warm, and the chair gently embraced Hali. The beach was empty, and the waves whispered in the background as the tide came in. Shorebirds waded in and out of the surf, their long beaks poking in and out of the sand as they gobbled down morsels that only they could see.

Mapenzie offered some fruit. "Harvested this morning." She took a piece of mango for herself and popped it in her mouth. "There are so many benefits to the changes that have swept our world. It baffles me that so many still choose to perpetuate fear."

"Fear becomes a habit. So much chaos and death make it hard for people to trust the good. People were screaming about the dangers of chemicals and the lack of cyber security for decades, and it turned out that much of what they feared came true. It may be a generation or two before people can accept the new world. That assumes that we have future generations."

Mapenzie nodded as she put down her coffee. "True. My great-granny was a child during the first Great Depression. My mother said that she'd become a hoarder as a result of her experience. She was so sure that the hard times would come again. She had a whole room just full of canned food."

"Yes, I've seen things like that. That's an understandable response to that kind of trauma. Sad, but understandable."

They sat silently for a moment, enjoying the fruit and the gentle breeze. Hali began, "Mapenzie, some of these conspiracy theories are so unbelievable that there's nothing I can say to dispute them. I can't give you evidence to dispute an unprovable negative. If people want to believe things like invisible beams aimed at their heads, you won't be able to convince them otherwise."

"I hear that, " Mapenzie replied, waving off the idea. "Some of the rumors are patently ridiculous. A small group is even convinced that MedPal isn't a semiplant but an alien race of body snatchers. That's clearly ridiculous. What about the idea that MedPal can alter brain chemistry and make people mindless zombies? That one is entrenched in the zeitgeist, one of the most repeated on my channel."

"That one is tough," Hali conceded, swirling her spoon through her steaming cup of tea. "Theoretically, if you can influence reproductive hormones, then you can affect the entire endocrine system. That would include brain chemistry. It would take evil intent or something drastically wrong, but I suppose terrible things are always possible."

"What could someone with evil intent do?"

Hali hesitated, not wanting to add to the fear-mongering. "You could do a lot of damage by messing with brain chemistry," she admitted. " Technically, you could chemically lobotomize someone or cause deep depression, manic behavior, or create addiction. Look at the role the reproductive hormones have on mood. The chemicals in our brains are much more powerful and color how we experience life."

She paused and looked around. "You probably understand the tech side better than I do. MedPal has future capabilities to alleviate depression, anxiety, addiction, and a whole host of other brain-related challenges, but it's not capable of any of that yet. That would be an entirely new capability that would have to be built from scratch in the code."

She took a sip of her tea. "People do a lot of damage with prescription drugs. They misuse their medications. The possibility of misuse with MedPal is zero. It's safer than giving someone a bottle of pills and relying on them to take them as instructed. MedPal takes the guesswork out of dosage and eliminates side effects by naturally helping the body produce the desired chemicals. When the time comes that we can use MedPal to help with diseases of the brain, it's going to be life-changing for many people. We aren't anywhere near there yet. MedPal is designed only to affect the reproductive hormones. Any anomalies would trigger an alert to the physician." She finished with conviction.

"Okay, so this one is an example of people taking a few tiny bits of truth and creating a monster from the pieces," Mapenzie acknowledged, her eyes searching Hali's. "But you're 100% sure none of that could be true? "

Hali nodded. "110%. There are too many safeguards in the program. In fact, one of my clients is married to one of the top execs at the firm. I can't disclose details, but I'll see them soon, and she'll be at the top of the list for the pre-launch."

"Good," Mapenzie smiled, her magnetic presence putting Hali at ease. "Now, let's talk about something more uplifting. Have you seen the new stand-up special with Robin Williams and Richard Pryor?"

As the conversation shifted to lighter topics, Hali's mind wandered. She'd never considered the nefarious possibilities. It was a good thing there were so many safeguards. She trusted the program. Everything was good.

===

Hali was surprised to see Emma's husband, Jared, with her for Emma's follow-up appointment. Hali greeted them with surprise, wondering why he'd come along. He was a patient; she'd also met him once or twice in her work with MedPal. He'd never come along to Emma's appointments.

"Jared, Emma, is something wrong?" Hali asked as she ushered them inside. "I've got you on the list for the MedPal. You should be getting your device in the next day or two."

Jared kept his voice light. "We're looking for other treatment options for Emma's depression."

Hali raised her eyebrows, glancing at Emma for confirmation. The confusion in Emma's eyes mirrored her own. "Is there a specific reason you oppose using MedPal for this, Jared?"

"I'd just like to try some other things first. I'm sure other people are in greater need of a MedPal."

"Well, there are other options like therapy, medication, and lifestyle changes," Hali suggested, trying to gauge Jared's reaction. "MedPal seems to be the best choice for Emma. In many cases, when you balance the reproductive hormones, it has a positive effect on mood. If it doesn't, I'll have much more information about what's happening. Many things can affect mood."

" I just don't think it's the right choice now; maybe in a few months," Jared replied.

Hali's brow furrowed. What was she missing? He was one of the critical people at Eos working on MedPal. It didn't make any sense. She wondered if something more was going on that he wasn't telling them.

"Let's talk about this. There are risks associated with any decision, even inaction. I'm surprised at your objection, Jared. I would think you'd be the first to recognize the benefits. You guys have been trying to get pregnant for seven years. What's going on?"

===

Jared ran a hand through his dark hair. It was probably nothing. Like Darin said, it was one small test run among thousands. They'd scrapped it. Still, the idea of something that he didn't trust, having access to his wife's body, was unacceptable.

"Okay," he conceded. "I'm sure it's nothing." He hesitated for a moment, Darin's warning echoing in his head. "But before the Crush, on the original version, some experiments were performed. I found the anomalous data and tracked it back."

Hali recoiled. "What kind of experiments?" Her tone was steel.

Jared realized he had no choice. A physician of her caliber wouldn't let it go. He should have prepared a better excuse. Risking Emma was not an option.

"This has to stay between us. This knowledge can be dangerous."

"I won't be part of any coverup or anything that violates my responsibility as a physician."

"It isn't like that. I've just learned that MedPal has some capabilities that I didn't know about. It's prewar stuff, not part of this version, but it's there."

"What kind of capabilities?"

"Alteration of brain chemicals."

Hali sat in shock, trying to understand what she'd heard.

Emma slammed her hand down on the table and jumped up, her eyes flashing angrily. "You LIED to me, Jared. You lied!!" She was vibrating with fury, her hands clenched in fists.

Jared tried to calm her. "I know, Em, I know. I didn't want to burden you. I didn't want to make things worse for you, but I couldn't let you get a MedPal until I get to the bottom of this. Please understand."

For a brief moment, silence reigned as they each tried to grasp the implications of the knowledge they now shared. Hali spoke first. "That is unacceptable, Jared. You need to stop the launch until we can assess the full parameters of what this means and how it could cause harm."

Jared nodded. "Believe me, that was my first instinct, too. But where does that leave us? Without an answer to our fertility issues, we're a dying species. I'm plugged into all the tech in the pipeline; we have nothing else in the works that will help. Do you have anything that has worked or is promising on the medical side?"

Hali covered her face with her hands and took a deep breath. She lifted her head and slowly shook it. "Nothing. Nothing at all. MedPal is our greatest hope. But how can we risk it?"

"How can we not?" Jared countered. "I've programmed an alert to tell me if the command sequence is triggered. I'll be watching, I promise."

"And if the alert triggers? What then? Do you have a plan to stop it?" Hali pressed him.

"Nothing concrete. Just the alarm so far. Let's pray that it never goes off. I'm trying to find a way to remove that function, but it's impossible without a major team effort. If word gets out, it could sink the whole project."

"It's a clear violation of the Accords! Why not just report it and let the AI monitors do something?"

"The monitors have scrubbed the program. If they showed nothing, it can only mean that there is corruption somewhere along the way. It would just mean that I would likely lose access, and then what?"

Emma fell heavily back into her chair. "Just another chapter in the who-gives-a-damn-about-ordinary people book! Just like the toxins they allowed in our food, water, and products before the Accords. Governments knew for decades that we were being poisoned, but they did nothing to stop it. It's not the AI that's evil; it's people! Dammit, Jared, we have to do something!" Her body trembled with rage.

Jared covered her hands with his. "I know, Em. I know." His voice was soft and soothing.

"I talked to Darin. He assured me that it was just experimental and that it was before the Accords. I know that's bullshit," Jared added. "I just found out a few days ago, and I don't know who to trust or what to do yet."

Hali stared at her hands, deep in thought. Her mind raced with questions and fears, thinking of all her patients and the potential for good and disaster. This was a nightmare. She felt like she'd felt at the worst of the pandemic. Useless, trapped in a nightmare, watching suffering unfold before her with no tools, no resources to help.

"Jared, I'll do whatever I can to help," Hali said. "I have access to patient data and firsthand experience with MedPal's effects. I can monitor my patients more closely and look for any signs of manipulation. This news is a disaster, but you're right. Stopping the MedPal rollout at this point would be a bigger disaster. We'll lose people's trust. We may lose humanity itself without an answer to the fertility crisis."

I'm digging deeper, but there's no fucking way Emma is going to wear that device. We've got to find a different way to help her."

Hali took a deep breath; the air in her small office felt thick and heavy with foreboding. She glanced at Jared and Emma, whose expressions mirrored her anger and resolve. The dim light from her desk lamp cast eerie shadows on their faces as a cloud passed over the sun, making the situation seem even more ominous.

"All right," Hali said, determination settling over her like a cloak. "I'm going to dig deeper into this. I'll search for any patterns or abnormalities in my patients' data. I haven't seen anything except great results, but now that I'm aware of the potential for problems, I'll look at things differently. Meanwhile, Emma, let's try you on some of the tried-and-true antidepressants."

With that, they gathered their belongings and prepared to leave the office. As the door clicked shut behind them, Hali paused momentarily, her gaze falling upon the framed Hippocratic Oath hanging on the wall. Had she already violated the oath of "do no harm?" Was she naive to embrace this leap forward without reservation? Indeed, enough of her colleagues had been hesitant. She should have listened.

Chapter 6: Meet the Nawers

Hali sat by her office window on the swivel chair, turning it from side to side. She couldn't sit still. Her hunched shoulders cast a distorted shadow across the floor. In the distance, half-finished construction projects stood like giant alien skeletons, the bones of buildings that would never be. They reminded her of how precarious future dreams could be. The warmth from the sunlight fought against the chill that crawled up her spine.

The MedPal pre-launch rollout was in its second week, and she was no closer to understanding the dangers it posed for her clients or how to mitigate them if they did occur.

"Dr. Bergero, your next patient is here," her assistant's voice echoed through the intercom, breaking her reverie.

"Thank you, I'll be right there," Hali replied, her tone steady despite the unease brewing within her. She glanced out at the quiet city before turning away from the window. How often did disaster loom while people went about their days, oblivious to the dagger hanging by a thread over their heads?

People walked or hovered by her window, doing their best to find normalcy in a world that looked much the same as before but was vastly different. Many more were still living mostly in their homes, coming out only when necessary. For a moment, Hali wished she had never pushed Jared to tell her the truth. As she walked down the hallway to meet her patient, Hali caught a glimpse of a headline on a news tablet: "MedPal: Savior or Saboteur?" She stopped to scan the article. It was just another conspiracy theory circulating online. They were growing more frequent as the technology became more pervasive. How much of it was true? How often had she read things that seemed outlandish and dismissed them without thought? After all, people had speculated about cyber warfare for decades but hadn't taken it nearly seriously enough.

"Good morning, Mr. Alget," She focused on her patient, allowing her empathy and compassion to push aside her doubts for the moment. As they discussed his medical concerns, Hali made a conscious effort to maintain eye contact and offer reassuring smiles – small gestures, perhaps, but ones she believed were vital in preserving the human connection in a world increasingly dominated by AI. "Remember, if you have any questions about your MedPal treatment, don't hesitate to call me," she said as their consultation ended.

"Thanks, Dr. Bergero. You're one of the good ones," He replied, his eyes brimming with gratitude.

Hali smiled, watching him leave the room before sinking into her chair, exhaustion washing over her. Was she still one of the good ones?

Grabbing her tablet, she scrolled through her social media feed, unable to escape the onslaught of MedPal-related content. There was an article suggesting that the true purpose of MedPal was to control the population by getting everyone addicted to

MedPal somehow. How do people know what is true and what isn't? Why couldn't the monitors do a better job of negating falsehoods? Living in the world today was like going to a David Copperfield show. You knew there was an illusion, but where was the illusion, and what was real?

"Dr. Bergero?" Her assistant peered into the room. "You have a call from your sister on screen two."

"Thank you." Hali activated the screen, hoping for a brief respite from the uncertainty that plagued her thoughts.

"Hey, Sarah! What's up? Are we still on for dinner?"

"Yeah. Aunt Jane is excited to see you. I'm her favorite, but for some reason, she thinks you're okay, too. Seven still good for you?"

"She just tells you that because she wants you to bring me because I'm her real favorite. The AutoAuto will pick us up at five."

"Great. Love you, Hali," Sarah replied before hanging up.

===

The AutoAuto picked Sarah up first, then Hali. "I still think we need a better name for autonomous vehicles," Sarah said after she'd greeted her sister. "How is it we've come so far with our tech and stayed so unimaginative with our naming of it? It reminds me of a company that held a naming contest for a new boat, and the winner was 'Boaty Boat McBoatface.

They had agreed to use the name that was most voted for, so they were stuck with it.'"

Hali smiled. Her sister was the creative one. Hali had always marveled at her ingenuity. "What would you call this?" she said, pointing to the vehicle they were riding in.

"I don't know. How about SteerClear? Or, Look, ma, no hands!" They laughed as the car moved silently down the street. Sarah kept going. "Hit and run? Pedestrians beware?"

Getting out of the city center took only fifteen minutes. During the Cyber War, everyone who stayed in the cities moved inward, looking to be close to where the supply drops were coming in, when they came. Hunger was a constant companion, and every calorie mattered. And nobody wanted to die alone.

Traffic wasn't a problem anymore. People didn't go out as much. The population was down, and the AI-assisted AutoAutos were efficient, so fewer cars were on the road. There were no speed limits. The car went to the maximum safe speed for the conditions.

As they began to drive through what had been the suburbs, the landscape changed dramatically. The veneer of homeyness was gone. None of the façade of normalness that the city had managed to regain was present. Here, the war had never ended and probably never would.

Houses were gaunt shells of what they had been, with broken windows and gaping doors left open from when they'd been looted for food and supplies as the war raged on. The suburbs had emptied as people chose city life or fled outward to practice self-sufficiency. Homes were stripped of everything valuable. Even doors and fences were taken for firewood so people could stay warm or cook food. Suburbia had become the moat between the city and the countryside, and the moat was full of unimaginable dangers. Feral people and pets roamed alongside wild animals that had reclaimed the territory humans had taken from them.

Just like the Japanese soldiers who refused to believe that WWII had ended, there were people in suburbia for whom the war might never end. Barely human, they resisted all attempts to help them. Drones dropped food and water, but the people broken by the horrors of disease and war would never recover. Like the Japanese soldiers who had lived their lives out in the jungle, fighting a war that had long since been over, these people would live in their hell until the mercy of death came for them.

Many of those who stayed had been poisoned in some way, some from the toxic smoke that blanketed the area as entire neighborhoods with homes full of pesticides and household chemicals burned. Others had poisoned themselves, drinking rubbing alcohol, washing themselves daily with a high concentration of bleach, or any of the other crazy things that people had believed would stop the Crush. Many people were injured by mixing cleaning products that created deadly fumes.

It didn't matter if the poisons had driven them mad or if the destruction of their world had broken them. They were broken beyond repair.

Politicians looking to appear as if they knew what to do had been perpetuating snake oil cures to get air time and pretend to be in control, and gullible people believed.

Pharmacies had been looted early on, and at the height of the madness, people paid a solid 24-karat gold bar for just one capsule of an antibiotic. Scammers were selling everything and calling it antibiotics. A fair number of men died with erections or found themselves growing breasts after taking birth control. If it was a pill, you could sell it as an antibiotic. Desperate people could be convinced of almost anything.

The landscape was apocalyptic. Homes were crumbling, their manicured lawns were overgrown with weeds, and mailboxes were lying in the street like dead soldiers. You could see the echoes of what had been in the rusty swing sets, algae-filled pools, and abandoned cars that littered driveways and yards.

In many places, driveways ended in a pile of blackened rubble where homes had burned down from ill-managed cooking fires or lightning strikes. In a world with no running water and no services, the smallest mistake could end you. Sarah pointed out a small campfire burning in the distance. "I can't believe people are still trying to live out here. It's so sad."

"For some, this will never end. We've sent help, but they refuse. Doctors for Hope sent out a team, but they got ambushed and sustained injuries." She sighed. " Nature is reclaiming this place. I guess that's a good thing." They passed an area where the entire subdivision was burnt out, with trees and bushes growing through the cement. The entry sign was untouched, ironically proclaiming, 'Welcome home to Sunny Acres!' A pack of wolves, wild dogs, or both howled in the distance.

Sarah shivered. "We took in a lot of refugees the first couple of months of the War, then they stopped coming. People realized early on that the choice was binary: go to the city and hope the government would remain functional enough to keep them from dying, or move out far enough to practice self-sufficiency. Most people made a choice, but others waited too long. They refused to believe that their perfect suburbs were death traps. The people that stayed here went through hell." Sarah's normal, irreverent tone was gone as the ghosts of the neighborhoods they drove through seemed to swirl around the car.

" How did you guys survive, even thrive, when suburbs were so hard hit?"

Even as she asked, Hali knew the answer. Rural communities cared for themselves and each other. They banded together and shared what they had. They created their own abundance and understood the interdependence of life. In suburbia, the illusion of community created by HOAs that cared about nothing but home values and appearances crumbled like the false homogeny of houses all painted in the approved color palette.

It was funny how people rarely talked about the Cyber War—nineteen long, brutal months. As if not mentioning it could negate what had happened. In the beginning, it wasn't so bad. There were intermittent outages, and some favorite foods were missing from supermarket shelves. People moaned about the lack of luxuries like coffee and chocolate but assumed it was temporary. Too many people had lived with peace and plenty for generations and didn't believe it could end. Living in denial until the end, they refused to change to meet how the world had changed. They weren't at all prepared for the violence that came when people got hungry enough. Suburbia had died a terrible death.

Like caged bunnies set free in a world of foxes, suburbanites had never seen the darkness that rose out of desperation. The world of door-to-door deliveries and Pilates classes imploded with a force that collapsed the complacency of many.

Others refused to believe, unable to imagine a world that wouldn't answer their every whim. They lamented the loss of their landscapers and house cleaners. Still, they couldn't fathom a world that didn't fit their ideals. They waited for the world to return to normal, for the next group of people to take care of the things that they considered beneath them. By the time they realized how wrong they were, it was too late.

The people from other countries recognized what was happening much sooner. They had lived among the foxes and wolves and tigers before. They had felt the sharp claws of hunger and seen the monsters that could be hatched inside the nicest people when their child was dying or what a person would do when the hunger pangs that they'd never experienced before gnawed their way through their guts and ate away their consciences.

Hali had seen it in emergency rooms as people fought for care for themselves and loved ones. Desperation could turn even the kindest person cruel. She turned to Sarah. "I was so glad that you stayed with Aunt Jane. I had to stay and do what I could. It made it easier, knowing you two were out here and as safe as anyone could be in that madness."

Sarah kissed her sister on the cheek, then laid her head on her shoulder. "I was so scared of losing you—nine months of not knowing if you were dead or alive. But Aunt Jane never faltered. She promised that you were okay and we'd see you again."

She put her arms around Hali, squeezing her tight. "She was right, and how she thinks is how most Nawers think. They don't look at the problems; they find the solutions. It's the reason the Nawers thrived, and suburbia died. I wish with all my heart you'd been with us. It was intense but also deeply transformative. As awful as it sounds to say it, those were some of the happiest days of my life." She pointed out the window.

"All those houses, filled with people who were strangers sharing a street. Sure, they might wave to each other or share a barbecue, but they didn't view their neighbors like Nawers do. Nawers see themselves as a community. If there's food for one, there's food for all. If one of them has a problem, everybody has a problem."

Sarah's infectious grin made Hali smile. "I lived without Twinkies for almost two years!" She laughed loudly, filling the car with the sound. Hali felt her heart lighten.

Her sister had always been able to make her laugh. Hali lived in a world of responsibility and burdens, and Sarah lived in a world of light and joy. "That makes all of the difference. Those who stayed at the hospital understood that each of us was vital. We held each other up when it felt like we would crumble under the weight of all the need."

"I know you don't like to talk about it, but I'm here if you ever want to. You try to protect me, but I'm a grown woman. You always try to take the full load. You can share it, you know. I can take it." Sarah took her hand, and they gazed out over the silent, eerie landscape. Every once in a while, they would pass a home still intact, looking like a live person trying to hide in a room full of zombies.

Hali whispered a prayer as they passed the last house. She knew all too well the stories of those homes. It had been much worse in the colder climates. Everything was stripped and burned. The Cyber War winter coincided with one of history's coldest, stormiest winters. Whole families were found later, frozen together in huddled masses. There were still bodies that might never be found.

As they left behind the bones of suburbia, the landscape transformed into rolling hills. The tattered remnants of suburbia gave way, and it felt like stepping back in time. The houses were smaller, the roads narrower. The buildings had a purpose. Barns and silos, feed stores-they all had a usefulness that was absent in other places.

Aunt Jane had lived in this small community in the foothills for as long as Hali could remember. She'd temporarily moved into the city when Hali needed help caring for her little sister while completing her residency. They'd all lived together in the family home that Hali had grown up in, but Jane would take Sarah out to her home in the country every chance they had. After a couple of years, it was clear that Jane and Sarah preferred the country.

Hali was sad but relieved when they all agreed on the move. She stayed in the city and went out as often as her busy life would allow her to spend her time off with them. As Sarah got older, that changed. It had been months since she'd been out to visit Aunt Jane.

As the rural areas organized themselves into communities, deserted buildings like Walmart and other abandoned mega-retail stores had been transformed into community centers, dormitories, and housing or recreation. People in the outlying areas had come closer, creating clusters of people that resembled villages of old. Somehow, they'd done something humans had been trying to do for a long time. They had a highly functioning society with equality and healthy interdependence.

Hali had been shocked at how much had changed. When she was finally able to come out after the Cyber War had ended, her aunt's quiet little town was a bustle of activity. Instead of the devastation she had feared, she found a thriving community. She had come to offer solace and healing to them and instead found it for herself. She wasn't surprised that her aunt had become a beloved elder. Aunt Jane had always been the wise woman who dried your tears and fixed everything with a cup of tea.

They had taken in more than three times their original population and somehow managed to feed and house them all. The old Walmart in the town center was the community hub, and the parking lots had been removed and replaced with gardens and fruit trees.

The strip mall that had housed the post office, the police department, and a few cafes and shops had been adapted to serve as the community kitchen and a place for people to offer things for trade.

There were still sagging barns and rusting tractors, but also cows and goats in pastures, and chickens, ducks, and turkeys wandered during the day, returning to their coops at night.

The whole area was an eclectic mix of old, new, and antique, including a set of Chippendale chairs found in the attic of an abandoned home and used in the community dining room. Before the Cyber War, they might have been worth hundreds of thousands of dollars. They were useful, and that's how they were valued to the Nawers.

They arrived at Aunt Jane's home, nestled among tall trees and surrounded by fragrant flowers. The chickens were fast asleep in their coops. The early twilight gave enough light for them to see the lush vegetable gardens and fruit trees heavy with fruit that had always been a hallmark of visiting Aunt Jane.

Jane had lived here for over forty years, and her unique touches were everywhere, from the grape arbor heavy with grapes leading up to her door to hundreds of homemade windchimes and mobiles made from reclaimed materials hanging throughout the gardens. Jane had used everything that came her way to create her art. Everything had a use in her eyes, from buttons and zippers to toothbrushes and plastic containers to old garden hoses and car parts.

A gentle breeze greeted them as they stepped out of the car, bringing the delightful sound of windchimes of every pitch and tone. The setting sun reflected from the yard art, sending sparkles of light dancing throughout the yard. As they walked past the small, Sweet Acacia trees on each side of the walk, they each raised a hand to the windchimes hanging from the branches. Hali's chime rang low and true, the heavy hollow wood stilling with a final, hardly audible note. Sarah's chime was light and chaotic as the different metals she had chosen came together at different speeds.

The door swung open before they could knock to reveal a beaming Aunt Jane, her arms flung open, as she rushed to hug them. She carried herself like a woman a decade younger than her sixty-four years. Her silver hair was pulled back in a loose bun with a bright green streak the color of a spring leaf on one side of her face. She was wearing her customary baggy pants and comfy t-shirt. They almost matched. They'd always joked that Aunt Jane wasn't color blind, she was fashion blind.

"Hali, sweetheart," Aunt Jane said, ushering them into the cozy living room. "It's been far too long." She sat down and poured the tea. The tea carried the scent of earth, like a freshly tilled field or the forest after a rain. "The quiche will be ready in about thirty minutes. While it bakes, you can catch me up on everything."

"This tea is heavenly!" Hali said, "And every time I come here, this town is more amazing."

"It's the meadowsweet," Aunt Jane said, pointing to the tea. It makes everything taste like a warm spring day." She pointed to a cheese tray on the simple homemade wooden table between them. "We have someone in town making cheese! Goat, cow, and sheep. Try it!" She lifted the plate towards them.

"And they have homemade wine!" Sarah said with a grin. "Pear, elderberry, and she makes a blueberry liquor that will knock you on your ass." Sarah stood up and stretched. "If you need me, I'll be out back doing quality control on the hammock."

Hali raised one eyebrow as her sister sauntered out. As soon as she left, Jane leaned in close. "I know something's up, Hali dear. I can read you like a book, and so can Sarah."

Hali sighed, a little more dramatically than the situation called for. She sipped her tea and leaned back. "Just like always, reading my mind. Sarah and I both used to think you were a witch."

Jane smiled, and her laugh lines turned her face into a mosaic of joyful beauty. "Used to? Ha! Come on, let's have it." She looked expectantly at Hali, her body language giving Hali no choice in the matter.

"I guess I just wanted to see you and see what you've been up to. And I have some concerns about MedPal. I've been a big proponent of it, but now I have doubts. I wanted your take on it. You've been cautious about AI from the beginning."

"Ah, MedPal." Aunt Jane's expression turned somber. "I can't say I'm surprised that there be some issues with it. Would you like to walk and talk? I think more clearly when I'm on the move, and I want to show you more of our life without AI. It's been a while since you've been here. We keep growing."

They walked out the front door. Hali rang her chime again like a talisman against everything she feared would happen.

Jane took Hali's arm as they walked the well-worn path along the road. "Everyone thinks that the Nawers - your term, not ours- sprang up overnight when the AI Accords were first drafted." Jane began as they strolled, "That isn't true. As early as the late 1990s, people sought a way back to simpler lives. The desire for a simpler, safer world grew when the first Covid lockdown happened. A lot of people changed their values. People began connecting through gardening groups, bread baking classes- all sorts of ways." She waved to a neighbor who was taking her laundry off the clothesline.

"By the early 20s, many people lived simpler lives in the cities and the countryside. By the time the AI Accords were signed, most Nawers knew how they wanted to live and had the skills to follow their choices. We still depend on the modern world and technology in many ways, but if things go bad, we'll be okay."

Hali stopped walking and turned to her aunt. "Go bad, how?"

Jane just shrugged. "So many things could happen. A strong sunspot, another Cyber War, AI getting so smart it decides we aren't worth the energy. You name it. Listen," she said, putting her arm around Hali and pulling her close. "We aren't gloom and doomers- just the opposite. We celebrate the incredible changes that AI has brought to our world. But history has taught us that given a chance, humans will find a way to mess up a good thing."

She paused and gestured at the pastoral scenes around them. Doors and windows were open to let in the gentle, scented breezes. People were relaxed, happy, and healthy. The few children they saw played happily together, some game that involved jumping over sticks and placing stones in strategic piles.

Technology wasn't absent. Some people moved about on hovers, and AutoAgs could be seen scurrying around gardens like giant insects tending their young. It was as if they had kept the best of the old-peaceful, connected living- and married it to the best of the new. It wasn't a life of labor; it was a life of love.

"This is paradise. But the world is full of people who see sinners where others see saints and those who see saints where others see sinners. We've found that the more resilient we are to the vagrancy of life, the happier we remain regardless of what the world does. So, we focus on being resilient, sustainable, and inclusive."

Hali nodded. She took a deep breath and plunged in before she could change her mind. "I need to tell you what I know." After she'd shared what she'd learned about MedPal, Hali waited anxiously for her aunt to berate her for her role in it all. They stopped to sit on a simple bench made from logs as Hali finished her tale.

Instead of berating her, Jane looked at her with wise, piercing eyes and spoke. "I guess the million-dollar question is who was behind the original test, and did they survive? Has someone found a way to circumvent the Accords, or was the command sequence AI generated? Are you fighting AI or humans?"

"I didn't expect you to be so pragmatic or to know that much about AI."

"I don't discard technology without trying to understand it. We don't disdain all tech. We're just careful about what we let in."

"We don't have the answers yet, but Jared is pretty sure it's human-driven, and they've managed to circumvent the Accords."

"The Accords were the only way to end the war. That doesn't mean people, especially those in power, are happy about it. Fundamentally, all the gatekeeping is being done by AI, with some human supervision, but we all know that people with money have found ways to circumvent the Accords. People in power know when to acquiesce to a superior force. Everyone agreed to the terms of the Accords because they had no choice. AI carved out brilliant compromises to end the war. A good compromise means everyone leaves the table unhappy in some way. I'm not naive enough to think those who lost some power will be happy about it. Of course, they'll try to get it back."

Hali took in the tranquil scenes. It was a far cry from the tech-dominated cities where people seemed more connected to their devices than each other.

"Everyone here has chosen to reduce reliance on AI," Aunt Jane continued. "We believe in preserving human autonomy and protecting ourselves from potential abuse. We've found a way to live that balances technology with the need for personal connection. Come on, let's go back before the quiche burns. I'll talk to some people over the next few days. Perhaps we can help. Many of our people are convinced that vigilance is our security and spend a lot of time learning what's going on in the world."

===

Later, back in the city, Hali walked into her home. Her AI greeted her as she entered. "Welcome home, Hali. Can I pour you a glass of wine? Would you like a hot bath?"

Hali felt a shiver run up her spine. The conveniences of her home had been a joy and a comfort. Usually, she'd relax in the bath and talk out her day with Chris, the name of her AI house interface. Now, everything felt different. "No, thank you," she said, heading to bed.

===

Hali sat at her desk, looking out the window. The afternoon rain streaked down the window, and the world seemed covered in gray. The clouds felt oppressive, bearing down on her.

Once again, she scanned the segmented patient report she'd run. Surely, she was reading it wrong. There were fifty-three couples on the fertility protocol. It had been two and a half months since the protocol started, and the MedPal report was telling her that twenty-four couples were in the early stages of pregnancy. Except they weren't. At least not all of them, that was for sure.

In the past week, Hali had examined seven women who were supposed to be pregnant. Based on Hali's physical exams, four of them were pregnant. Three most definitely were not, but still appeared on her list. Based on how far along MedPal had indicated the pregnancies were, there should be physical changes that were clear signs of pregnancy. The physical exams hadn't shown these signs, but MedPal was transmitting results that unequivocally indicated pregnancy.

Most doctors participating in the MedPal beta test were not physically seeing patients. They were doing everything with Telemed and the MedPal data. For Hali, seeing patients was the most essential part. She would be obsolete if it were just about transmitting results, adjusting levels, or suggesting lifestyle changes. Being a physician was more than that. It was being a trusted advisor and confidante and giving patients a safe place to express their concerns.

It was obvious that MedPal was manipulating data to make results appear more successful than they were. How much of MedPal data was a lie? Were they lying about just fertility results? She'd measured patients on other metrics, like AIC, blood pressure, and pulse rates, which matched perfectly. Was the fertility program a trojan horse meant to create a sense of safety and progress? Were they trying to cover up poor results, or was something more sinister at work? She needed to meet with Jared.

Jared answered her text immediately. "I have news also." Meet me at the coffee vend near the park."

===

Hali watched as Jared approached. He walked with the confidence of someone in peak physical condition, his eyes ever scanning the world around him.

"Want something?" Jared asked as he pressed his index finger on the vend screen, then touched it again to confirm that he'd like his usual green matcha tea with coconut milk.

"No thanks."

The vend placed his drink on the counter with a cheery "Thank you for drinking from Starry Vend!" He grabbed it and turned back to Hali.

"Let's walk." They walked along the sidewalk that curved through the park. The rain had stopped, but the clouds remained. Water still dripped from trees, and the bushes seemed to crowd closer as if to hear what they had to say.

"I got an alert today. I checked it. It's a person in Paris. She's on the beta test. Lately, she's been advocating on social media for us to slow down the rollout and slow AI advancement in general. She's got a couple million followers, so she's made a bit of a splash." His face turned grim. "At least she had. The alert was triggered first thing this morning. By lunchtime, she was singing the praise of MedPal and all AI again."

Hali shared her information about the fertility data. They walked in silence, both digesting the implications of the news that the other had shared.

Hali spoke first. "We need more information and more help. I know someone that might be able to help."

Mapenzie had just finished her morning broadcast when they arrived. As they walked in, Jared looked around at the screens that covered every wall while autonomous robots were busy cleaning, cooking, and working outside trimming in the lush gardens. "This house looks like an AI advert."

"I made my brand by reporting on AI. I've tried all the AI-enhanced tech, from the first kitchen bots to the top-of-the-line companion bots. In the beginning, I had to invest everything I made back into buying the newest thing, but now, all the AI and tech companies send me every new thing they make. I've got boxes I haven't had time to open yet."

She pointed out the window at the humanoid robots trimming the trees. "Those don't need to be humanoid at all. You can buy garden hoverbots that will do everything that these do and for a lot less money. But it turns out that people want their robots to look human."

Jared nodded. "It's incredible how far the humanoids have come. I've interacted with some and would have sworn I was talking to a person. If the Accords didn't require that humanoids self-disclose, we'd be even more vulnerable."

"Don't get too complacent about the self-disclose reg. I've heard that there's a hack to get around that."

"What else do you know about Accord violations?" Hali asked.

"Why do you ask?" Mapenzie looked suspiciously at Hali. "You didn't come here to chat about bots."

"We have some concerns about MedPal," Jared answered her.

"Concerns?" Mapenzie asked. Tilting her head and narrowing her eyes, she spoke directly to Hali. "Didn't we already have this conversation? What could be wrong? Didn't we agree that MedPal was revolutionizing wellness? "

"We need to tell you some things," Hali replied

When they'd finished, Mapenzie was furious. "Millions of people trust me. I've been advocating for AI technology since the beginning. How do I know that you aren't just buying into some of the conspiracy bullshit?"

"Don't you think I want it to be bullshit?! I'm heading up the team that's overseeing the rollout. This isn't a fucking conspiracy. I saw it with my own eyes." Jared vibrated with anger to match Mapenzie's.

Hali spoke calmly. "This isn't helping. You're getting angry at the wrong people. We need to find a way to dig deeper. Mapenzie, you've got a direct line to millions of people. We need to find some people who know more."

"The Musky principle. *If tech can be used for evil, then evil men will seek that tech*. We need to find the people who answer to the second part of that principle." Jared interjected.

Mapenzie nodded. *"If tech can be used for good, then good men will seek that tech.* We need to find those good people. Despite the sexist nature of that quote, I believe it to be true. It's always the person wielding the tool that's the problem. So, what do we do now?"

"Get proof. I'm going to schedule exams with all the women that MedPal says are pregnant and find out how many are a lie."

"I need to access the data of the woman who set off the alert and find out exactly what it did to her," Jared added.

"And me? I'm not going to keep telling people to wear a MedPal!"

"Everyone knows you take a tech fast from time to time. Take one now, and then try to find out if any commenters on your videos talking about the conspiracy theories have any real information." Hali urged. "Conspiracy theories usually have a kernel of truth somewhere. If we can find that kernel and the person who has it, they might lead us to something."

Mapenzie spun around the room, taking in the technology surrounding her, and shuddered. "I can't take a tech fast here. Sarah has been bugging me to meet your Aunt Jane for years. I think it's time to do that."

"Great idea." Hali agreed.

"I'd like Emma to get out of town too. I don't want her to worry; she'll try to help. I can't risk her." Jared added.

"Let me call Aunt Jane. She has plenty of room and loves having people around to dote on."

Chapter 7: Discovered

The cold wind blew through the broken windows of the deserted warehouse, rustling discarded papers and debris. Shadows flickered as the faint glow of moonlight filtered in from outside. Hali shivered, pulling her coat tighter around her slender frame. "This place gives me the creeps, Jared. Why are we here?"

"In the three days since we visited Mapenzie, something has shifted at Eos. I don't think it's safe to be seen together, and that's why we're here," he replied, his voice echoing in the cavernous building.

He rubbed his hands together for warmth, dark eyes darting back and forth as if expecting danger to jump out at any moment. "Nobody comes out to these old warehouse districts anymore. Something's not right, and I can't shake the feeling that someone's been watching me since my conversation with Darin. I don't want to endanger you."

"Have you found anything concrete?" Hali asked.

"Nothing yet.," he admitted, frustration evident in his tone. "But something's off. We're missing a piece of this puzzle and we have to find it before more people get hurt. What if we're wrong, and the mind control experiments are about something else? There's something going on here that we aren't seeing. The alert hasn't triggered again, but I still don't know what exactly MedPal did to that woman and, more importantly, who triggered the command sequence for her MedPal. I need you to examine the report and explain the medical stuff to me."

He glanced around again, bouncing on the balls of his feet as if he were ready to fight an invisible opponent. "I'm trying to trace it back, but we need to be vigilant as hell."

Hali sighed, running her fingers through her hair. "I agree. My patients trust MedPal with their lives, and I'm the one who talked them into it. We need to fix this before someone else gets hurt."

Jared nodded. "Then let's figure this out. We'll start by going over everything we've learned so far. What doesn't add up? What questions still need answers?"

"I think you need to talk to my Aunt Jane. The Nawer communities have resources and aren't connected to AI." A distant sound interrupted her. "What was that?"

The eerie silence of the warehouse enveloped them. The once bustling industry hub now stood as a haunting reminder of the past, its disrepair casting an ominous shadow over their clandestine meeting. Stripped of paint and marred by age, the walls loomed menacingly above them, and the shadows were filled with menace. The distant hum came again, a little louder.

===

The faint buzzing sound echoed through the cavernous building, growing louder by the second. Jared and Hali exchanged wary glances as they realized they were no longer alone. Emerging from the shadows, a group of sleek drones appeared, their sinister designs leaving no doubt that their purpose was enforcement. They swiveled ominously toward the pile of blue plastic barrels Hali and Jared stood behind. Evil-looking turrets rose from their center.

"Fuck! They must have followed me," Jared hissed, his eyes narrowing as he assessed the situation. "We need to move, Hali. Now!"

The drones began firing their bullets at the barrels they were standing next to. "Go!" They ran toward the back of the warehouse, bullets flying from the drones as they desperately scrambled for safety.

"I don't think they're trying to kill us. If they were, we'd already be dead!" Jaren panted. As the drones closed in, they swiftly maneuvered through the maze-like layout of the warehouse, dodging obstacles and narrowly avoiding gunfire.

"Over here!" Jared shouted, spotting a narrow passage between two giant wooden crates. He led Hali through the tight space to an opening between some pallets. A forklift stood nearby; the fork partway lifted as if it had stopped in the middle of something.

"Jared, duck!" Hali warned as a drone swooped in, attempting to corner them. Thinking quickly, she grabbed a nearby metal rod and swung it at the drone, knocking it off course and buying them precious time.

"Nice shot, Hali," Jared said, grinning despite the danger. "That's one down."

"Thanks," she replied, panting slightly from exertion. "But we can't celebrate just yet. We need to keep moving."

"Agreed," he said, eyes scanning the area for their next move. "If we can make it to the other side of the warehouse, we might be able to find a way out."

"Let's do it," Hali panted, steeling herself for the continued chase.

Together, Jared and Hali moved through the warehouse. Splinters of wood and debris flew through the air as the gunfire shredded the crates and barrels they tried to take cover behind.

===

"Wait, hold on," Jared said suddenly, pulling Hali behind another stack of wooden pallets as a drone swooped past. "I've got an idea."

"What?" Hali asked.

"I need just a few seconds to jam their signals." Jared pointed to one hovering nearby, its sleek design and advanced weaponry menacing even from a distance. "I think I can disable them. That way, we can study it later and learn more about who's controlling these things. Put some faces to our enemies."

"You can do that? " Hali questioned.

"Yep," Jared replied tersely as more bullets ripped into the pallets they were hiding behind.

"I'll lead them away," Hali grabbed the metal rod she had used earlier and ran back out into the line of fire.

The bullets ripped the air around her as she dodged from one hiding place to the next. She felt something burn her shoulder as she stumbled over a small pile of stones. As she fell, she knew this was the end. She closed her eyes against the bullets. They never came. The sudden silence filled her with relief as she rolled over. He must have done it. Jared ran over to her.

"You're hit!" He exclaimed as he knelt by her side. She grimaced and wiped off the blood trickling down her shoulder.

"Just a scratch. You did it! How?"

"I have a jammer on my phone - I just needed to find their frequency. This will only buy us a little bit of time. Whoever is behind this will send more or key in a different frequency. We need to go. Can you make it?"

Hali looked down at herself. Her palms were scraped from the fall, her shirt was torn and bloody, and she'd landed badly on some rocks and felt the bruises already forming. "Yeah, I'm okay. Let's go."

As they left the warehouse, Jared grabbed one of the disabled drones. "We need to find out who's behind this," he said. I need to know if there's anyone I can still trust at Eos.

He opened the casing, pulled out a part, and threw it aside. "They won't be able to trace it. It will show as DBR- damaged beyond repair- and they won't attempt to recover it."

Hali said, "Let's meet at Aunt Jane's in three hours. We'll take separate routes to throw anyone off our trail." She shared the GPS coordinates and cautioned him, "You'll need to download this route. You'll lose the GPS signal about fifteen minutes from the community, and there are a lot of turns afterward. Depending on where in the community you are, you could have anything from no WIFI up to 4G. Everything 5G and higher won't be available."

"Let me do something first," Jared said as he connected his phone to her AutoAuto. His fingers danced over his screen, and her car beeped an acknowledgment. "Your car now shows that you went to your office and out to Milly's for lunch, stopped at the gym, and then went home. That's what will transmit to the hub. I should have thought to do that as soon as we arrived."

"You are full of surprises. Is there anything you can't hack?"

"Let's hope not. Be careful!" He jogged away, the drone in one hand and the other holding his phone, his thumb flying across the screen.

===

Hali arrived at Aunt Jane's in the dusk of early evening. Jared had arrived just a few minutes prior. Sarah and Mapenzie were out walking. Emma and Jared held each other like they'd been separated for weeks instead of days.

Jane rushed forward. "You're hurt! I felt something was wrong!"

Hali hugged her. "I'm fine, Aunt Jane. Just a few bumps and bruises."

They gathered on the back patio. Jane tended to Hali with medicinal salves and a cup of chamomile and lavender tea to soothe her nerves. The fire flickered warmly under the full moon as Jane poured the homemade blueberry liquor into their glasses. " Hey, how come I'm drinking tea while you guys drink the good stuff?" Hali joked

"Are we still on planet Earth?" Mapenzie quipped as she walked onto the patio. This place is fantastic!"

Her light demeanor shifted as she hugged Hali. "What the hell happened to you?"

Hali winced from the hug. Despite her best efforts to clean up, her face was scratched, and she couldn't hide the stiffness in her body. She smiled weakly. "You should see the other guy." She gestured to the drone lying on the side table.

After Jared and Hali shared their news, Mapenzie stood up. "I haven't found anything concrete either," she admitted, "but one of my followers has been very cloak and dagger." She sipped her blueberry liquor and leaned against the ornately carved wooden sideboard.

"Whoever they are, they claim to have been an employee of a tech billionaire. They wouldn't say which one. According to them, they know of a plot to reduce the world population so that a select group can own the world or something. It's a group calling themselves the 144. I'm trying to meet with him to find out more."

Jane gasped, and her face turned white-green, making her seem almost like the plants that surrounded her. They all turned to her. She sat on the couch with her hand on her chest and her eyes open wide like a startled doe. "It can't be. It can't."

"What?" Mapenzie urged. "Tell us."

"Give me a moment. I have to think." After what seemed like hours to the others but was just a few seconds, she began to speak. "You have to understand. I have listened to rumors for decades. There was always a new apocalypse on the horizon. Secret societies, aliens, and comets portending the end of the world. I thought this was just one more collective delusion, like when some people thought the Covid vaccines had trackers in them-things like that are always part of the zeitgeist."

She stopped and took a sip of her blueberry liquor. "Twenty-seven years ago, I had an affair with a married man. He worked for Lonny Zebum."

"Lonny Zebum, the man who united all the old tech companies to form Eos?' Jared asked

"Yes. Of course, at the time, he was still head of MicroAp. I'm not proud that I fell in love with a married man, but hearts will do what they will do. We met at a Herbal Conference, of all things. He was trying to find his way back to nature and a simpler life."

Hali and Sarah both raised their eyebrows, surprised by all of this. Mapenzie noticed and thought of how similar their mannerisms were, even if they didn't look much like sisters. Jane continued. "He had children, so after a few wonderful months, we agreed that we needed to stop for the sake of his family. I didn't hear from him for several months. Then he called me out of the blue and asked me to meet him at a cabin belonging to his friend up on the mountain. He sounded desperate."

"I almost didn't go, but he sounded so frightened and unlike himself that I felt I had to." Jane's eye glistened with unshed tears. Her voice was husky with emotion. "He was raving when I got to the cabin. He wasn't making any sense, and he claimed that someone was trying to kill him for what he knew. He begged me to tell everyone what he was telling me, to go to the media and post it everywhere to stop it. I wasn't sure what "it" was. He was pretty incoherent." She took a deep breath.

"His wife showed up a few minutes after I did with a couple of male nurses. She knew who I was and wasn't happy to see me. She explained that her husband- and she made sure to stress that phrase- her husband- had an inoperable brain tumor and was no longer capable of caring for himself. It had progressed, and all they could do was keep him comfortable. I left as they were giving him medication. I'll never forget his face that day. He locked eyes with me, and the desperation I saw almost broke me. Those eyes, imploring me to believe him, stayed with me all these years. Now you're telling me that he wasn't mad, that I should have done something."

"I'm so sorry, Aunt Jane," Hali murmured, picturing the awful scene. "But what does that have to do with this?"

"He died shortly after that, and for all these years, I believed that he was out of his mind when he told me those things. Until yesterday. Even then I didn't really believe it."

"What happened yesterday?"

"Yesterday, I heard a story from a credible source while I was digging for information. I didn't want to believe it, but what you're saying makes me know it is true. Too many people are telling the same story. It was so close to what James had been saying that awful night that I wondered if James had been murdered -if what he was saying was true. When you mentioned the 144, I knew it had to be true. He kept imploring me to stop the 144. I thought it was just ravings. I probably would have been killed, too, had I believed him and tried to do something. Or maybe I could have saved him."

She looked down at her hands as if seeing the blood of her dead lover on them. "And now you've just confirmed it. James said we had to stop the 144 before it was too late. My Gaia, what have I done?"

"You have to tell us all of it, Aunt Jane." Sarah exploded out of her chair and began pacing. "We need to know what we're facing so we can *do something.*"

Jane nodded. "James was out of his mind, so I don't know how much of what he told me is real. They must have done something to his brain. Here are the parts of the story he told me that agree with what I heard yesterday." She nodded at Jared and Hali. "And what agrees with what you're telling me."

"I think we're just looking at the tip of an iceberg of evil. Here's what I've heard from several sources. A group calling themselves the 144 plans on taking over the world, and the rest of us are in the way. They want the entire world for themselves, and the rise of tech makes it feasible for them. They knew that AI and robotics would create a new world. They want to own that world. Like much of the evil that man creates, they've perverted the writings of the bible. They believe the world needs a cleansing that will allow the earth to regenerate and become heaven for them and their offspring. From what I learned yesterday, Eos is central to the plan."

"Eos!?" Emma asked. "The same company my husband works for? Is this some kind of joke?"

Jared grimaced. "I wish it was, Emma. The drones that tried to kill us are military grade, and the hardware is from Eos. I suspect that the only reason we're still alive is that Darin may be trying to protect me. Or it could be that he's the one who ordered me to be followed. I don't know who or what to trust anymore."

Mapenzie grimaced impatiently. "Hey! I need to hear everything, *now*! Are you telling me that all these crazy conspiracy theories are true? And that you- and you- and especially you believe them?" She pointed first at Hali, then Jared, then Sarah.

They each nodded in turn, then turned expectantly to Jane.

"Think about the history of the world," Jane began. "Societies have always been pyramids—a precious few at the top live lives of extraordinary luxury.

Depending on what time in history you are talking about, this could be as simple as having the biggest tent, the best food, and many wives. Or it could be as extreme as the lavish and reckless lives of the billionaires on the planet now."

She paused to sip the smooth liquor that sparkled in her glass. "The one constant through all this is that the people on the bottom are the ones that supply all the labor for all the things that the ones on the top enjoy. The disparities between the top and the bottom are always great, but the people at the top are always aware of their vulnerabilities. There is more dependence in these relationships than they want to admit."

Jane crossed and uncrossed her legs, looking to calm the restlessness of the memories. "You might have heard the term 'Bread and Circuses.' It refers to the idea that to keep the masses from rising in revolution, you must keep them fed and entertained." In a voice so hushed that it was almost a whisper, Jane leaned forward and said: "What happens when the people at the top no longer need the people at the bottom? What happens when all the labor is AI and robotic?"

Hali looked at her incredulously. "Are you saying what I think you're saying? You can't be..." Her voice trailed off.

Mapenzie jumped up and began to pace again. "You better spell this out for us. Are you really suggesting some global elite group is planning to murder everyone on the planet? And MedPal is the vehicle they'll use to do it?"

"Not quite in the way you're thinking, but the result will be the same. From what I've gathered, the plan will unfold over the next several decades. It's a combination of suppressing fertility while accelerating diseases that lead to early death. They believe that the singularity is here and that they will be immortal. Rumors abound on how they expect to be immortal, but clones and memory transfer are the most persistent rumors."

"Fuck! Fucking MOTHERFUCKERS! Goddamn fucking monsters! We need to find them and wipe their fucking elite fucking useless asses off the fucking planet for good!" Sarah's explosion of anger startled them all.

Mapenzie grabbed her by her upper arms and held her still. "That won't help. We need to be smart; we need to be strong, and we need to be in control. Running off without a game plan is just suicide."

She turned back to Jane. "What else do you know?"

"Not much for certain. Rumors abound in our community. A lot of people in our community have been exploited and discarded- they have little faith in safety or the largesse of society. Until yesterday, I ignored the rumors, thinking they were the usual fear-based mutters of angry and disenfranchised people. I've heard them all, though. The most persistent ones revolve around MedPal. It's a soup of madness– they're going to use MedPal to sterilize the entire population. They're going to use MedPal to kill everyone over sixty and then have everyone else die as they turn sixty. They're going to use MedPal to control our minds, so we sit in the corner and die. They're going to give us all heart attacks. You know how it is—too much noise to tell what's real and what isn't. James did mention mind control several times. I wish I'd listened." Her tears spilled over. Hali held her hands while the tears streamed down.

Emma turned to face Jared. "Could this be why we've never gotten pregnant? Could they be behind the infertility crisis? Jared, you have to do something! None of us understand the tech like you do."

Hali interjected. "Emma, there are many reasons people aren't getting pregnant these days. Toxins in our environment play a big part, and sperm counts have been falling for decades in the developed world. But it seems clear that if this is true, then MedPal is going to be an instrument of their atrocities."

"And who creates the toxins? The global elite who run the corporations." Emma spat out, her anger contorting her beautiful face.

"Is there anything else that you know?" Hali asked Jane, with her usual calm control.

"That's it. I think. The 144 refers to the 144 thousand people from the Book of Revelations. They believe that their wealth and power are the seals proving their worthiness. They think we're already in end times, and they are the tool of God, facilitating a return to heaven on earth. With them as the new gods. They think they are the chosen ones and will live forever. They think that heaven on earth is their birthright. Anyone who isn't in their group will die."

Everyone sat in shocked silence, disbelief written all over their faces.

"That's not possible- on so many levels!" Hali blurted out. "Just the idea of that many dead makes the world unworkable. Look at what it costs us to lose thirty percent of the population. The world couldn't function. Cities would be full of dead bodies. Whole areas would be unlivable. There are still almost seven billion people on the planet!"

"If you have the whole planet as your playground **and** immortality, then all these things become irrelevant. AI is filling the gaps that have been left by the people we've lost already. There is no need for anyone to clean, build, farm, produce, massage, drive, or do any of the other things that are now able to be done by AI bots."

Jared stood up. "She's right. Even the world's oldest profession is no longer necessary. Look where we are: thirty percent of the population is gone and declining steadily. What if they've already started? What if the Crush and the Cyber War were designed to make the MedPal readily adopted?"

"So, what do we do?" Sarah interjected. "Past is past. How do we stop them?"

"We need to expose them!" Mapenzie declared. "I need to tell my followers!"

"It's still too dangerous, and you'll just sound like all the other conspiracy theorists." Sarah protested vigorously. "Plus, you can't post from out here."

"Then I'll go back into the city limits to post the videos," Mapenzie insisted. "If I save one person, it's worth it. I convinced millions that MedPal was safe. I won't be responsible for the death of people who trusted me!"

"Absolutely not!" Emma protested, gripping Mapenzie's arm. "It's too risky. You can't trust anyone right now. What if Eos finds you?"

"I appreciate your concern, but I'm not afraid," Mapenzie replied, gently removing Emma's hand from her arm. "This is bigger than us, and I won't let fear hold me back. I have to do something- I'm the one who kept telling everyone how great it would be. We must do something now; this is our best shot at making a difference. We aren't ready to stop them, but I can slow them down. Enough people will believe me to make a difference. It's a start."

Jared, Hali, and Aunt Jane exchanged glances before nodding reluctantly. Mapenzie had a point, and her influence could indeed help their cause.

"Fine," Hali sighed. "But you need to be extremely careful."

"Promise," Mapenzie agreed.

"We need more help," Jared said. "I'm going to phone a friend."

"Who?" Hali asked

"Adam Besus"

"Wait! What? The billionaire that became a recluse a decade or so ago? Fell completely off the radar?" How can you be sure he isn't one of the 144?"

"I can't be sure, but if he is, then we're fucked. He's a good guy. I don't believe he'd be part of this. He's our best shot at getting somewhere. He's been a tech mover and shaker like nobody else. He gave away most of his wealth when he went underground a year or two before the Crush, but he'll still know all the players. We need someone like him."

Chapter 8: Adam and Daniella

Jared stood by the bench; his stillness was almost supernatural. The park was empty, Birdsong filled the air.

Hali sat on the bench, her arms crossed over her chest against the chill in the air. "What are you hoping to get from this guy?"

"He might be able to lead us to Motisha Sukoki. She wrote the base code for all AI. If anyone can help us, it's her."

Hali nodded doubtfully. "Is that even a real person? Satoshi Nakamoto was the supposed founder of Bitcoin, and people have been looking for him for decades. "

"She's real," Jared said. "If she's not, we're all fucked."

"You think this man will know where she is? If Motisha is even a she. From what I hear, there's been more sightings of her than Elvis and Michael Jackson combined."

Jared gave an exasperated sigh. "I don't know what Adam knows or doesn't, but he can help us. He's got resources and contacts and is one of the smartest guys I've ever met."

"How do you know him?"

Before he could answer, a man stepped out from the bushes behind them. He was well over six feet tall, his stature commanding attention. Dressed in a blue plaid shirt and jeans, he appeared more like a lumberjack than a genius entrepreneur. His face bristled with a wild beard, a beard braid adorning the center and hanging to the middle of his muscular chest. Jared looked like a child next to him.

"What's up?" Adam greeted them with a friendly smile, at ease despite the circumstances. "All this cloak and dagger shit, Jared, it seems intense. I always wanted to be James Bond."

"Adam," Jared said with relief. "Thanks for coming, man. I wasn't sure you would."

"Ah," Adam replied, tugging his beard braid like a secret handshake while his eyes danced with irreverence. "Brothers in blood and all that other fraternity shit. Of course, I came."

Hali raised an eyebrow, not impressed by the man before her. "You seem pretty laid back about this all."

Adam chuckled again, his eyes twinkling with amusement. "I don't know what 'this all' is. I'm just answering the call of a fraternity brother." He turned to Jared. "Okay, give it to me. What have you gotten yourself into?"

By the time Jared finished, Adams' eyes were no longer twinkling. "Do you know why I gave it all up and walked away?"

Jared and Hali both shook their heads.

"Rishard Feller tried to get me to join a club he was in. I was still in the game and looking to fund the expansion, so I went to a dinner he hosted. It was like I was in a Steve Berry novel. They were talking about the singularity and the importance of "intelligent" men and women controlling all the tech in the world. I suspect that had I expressed interest, I would have learned more. I found it ridiculous and frightening. Too many people in the room thought they had the right to run the world. That's when I realized I didn't want any part of that world." He paused, then looked pointedly at Jared. "You have a plan?"

"Not yet. We need one more person. I think you know who I mean." Jared waited for Adam to reply.

"Fuck! Yeah, we do need her. Do you know how to find her?"

"I think so. I know where she was a couple of years ago. She's not one for a big change, so she's probably still there."

"Hopefully, she's still firmly anti-violence. Otherwise, she might shoot me on sight." Adam said ruefully.

===

The coffee shop was warm and airy, with bright lighting and sleek chrome fixtures. Adam scanned the room, settling on the slender figure hunched over a tablet in the corner. She was absorbed in her work, fingers drumming impatiently on the table as if she were composing an intricate symphony. Her birdlike appearance, delicate features, and sharp, intelligent eyes made her seem fragile. One of the most brilliant minds today lay beneath her unassuming exterior: Daniella Misern.

Adam stared at Daniella, his eyes narrowing as he looked at her. "She looks the same. Maybe she's mellowed over time."

Jared snorted. "You hope!"

The three of them approached Daniella, who slowly raised her head from her tablet, her fingers still tapping their restless rhythm. It took a moment, but her fingers stilled when she recognized the man under the beard.

Surprise, puzzlement, hope, and anger flitted over her face before it settled into a cold, emotionless mask. "What are you doing here?" her voice was almost a hiss, the words spilling out like she couldn't stop them. "I have nothing to say to you, and I don't want to hear anything you say." She turned back to her tablet, her fingers resuming their restless beat.

Hali stepped forward. "Hi. I don't know what the history is here with you two. I'm Dr. Hali Bergero, and we desperately need your help. We need to talk privately."

Jared leaned in closer, lowering his voice. "We're trying to find Motisha Sukoki."

Daniella's fingers paused their drumming for a moment, her eyes narrowing. "You and the rest of the planet, buddy. Nobody even knows if she exists. She could be anyone. Or a figment of someone's imagination."

"I hate to be cliche," Jared replied, his voice steady. "But the fate of the entire planet may rest on us finding her." He remembered the last time he had said that same thing. He didn't really believe it when he'd said it before. Now he knew it was a terrible truth.

Daniella studied them momentarily, her gaze flicking between Jared, Hali, and Adam. She seemed to be weighing their sincerity. "Follow me."

Jared exhaled, relief flooding through him. "Thank you, Daniella." They followed her brisk steps to an innocuous door at the back of the cafe. "I like my privacy, but sometimes I think better in a room full of people."

The door unlocked as she placed her eye on a small scanner recessed at just the right height for her eye. It blended with the wall and could hardly be seen. They entered a well-lit room slightly bigger than the coffee shop. Several screens covered the walls, and three workstations were spread throughout the room. Ergonomic chairs were scattered throughout. One corner had a beige leather sectional with soft, welcoming pillows and cozy blankets. A pair of fuzzy slippers sat on the ottoman, looking forlornly out of place in the high-tech environment.

"Still have cold feet?" Adam said, looking down at her in a way that might have been longing. Daniella glared at the clear double entendre and didn't reply.

She punched several buttons on a panel by the door, then pointed to a round table. "All the WIFI and AI-assisted tech is off in this room now. Sit. I'll give you ten minutes."

Hali waved her hand at the room around them. "You own the cafe? And this is your office?"

"Like I said, sometimes I like privacy, sometimes I like people. Start talking."

As Jared laid it out for her, she gave Adam a bitter look. "It's a shame that nobody could foresee the problems that AI might bring. Too bad nobody advocated for controls."

At her sarcastic words, Adam put his head between his hands. "I know, Daniella, I know. What can I say? We were young and dumb and full of ourselves. We thought we were saving humanity. We thought that once we solved the problems of hunger, war, and lack, man's better nature would blossom. I'm sorry I didn't listen to you. It appears you were right. Is that what you need to hear?"

Daniella gave a deep sigh. "You have no idea how much I wish I were wrong. I believed you guys had done it and that the world was on its way to experiencing a Renaissance that would lead us into a golden age. After the Accords, I really thought I'd been wrong. I get it, Adam. Eventually, I drank the Kool-Aid too."

She shot out of her chair so rapidly that it rocked back and knocked into a waste basket. The questions started as soon as she stood up. "Why Motisha? What's the plan? Do you even have a plan? Or are you still doing the leap before you look thing that you were so famous for at Harvard?" Her questions came like gunfire, and every one of them seemed aimed at Adam.

"Come on, Dani. You can beat me up later." Adam joked lightly, trying to break the tension.

Jared jumped in. "You must have heard the rumors that she put a back door in the original code that only she can access. Her code has been the foundation of every AI since the beginning. It's everywhere, from ChatGPT to the AI systems running the world. If we can find that backdoor in MedPal, we can stop them."

Daniella nodded. "I'm willing to hear more. But you'll need a team to get anywhere near the place where you'd have to open the backdoor if it exists. If Motisha even exists. Do you have one?"

Jared nodded. "I think so."

"That's a start." She grabbed a bag from a nearby workstation and pointed towards the door.

"I'm assuming you have a more secure spot. Turning off AI and Wi-Fi in the middle of the city leaves a hole that sooner or later they'll want to investigate."

"Just like that?" Adam asked. "You'll come with us?"

"Just like that." She agreed firmly.

===

Jared was surprised by the room. He expected to be stepping back in time when he met with the man who had been instrumental in uniting all the disparate communities into the cohesive Nawer movement. The touchscreen covering the entire wall of his office wasn't what you'd expect from a man who'd united people all over the globe under the banner of low tech-no tech.

The room was light and modern but with touches that seemed to evoke a simpler time. The lamps still had switches. The fans had pulls. It was clear that voice-activated tech wasn't available in this room. Hali stepped forward and offered her hand. "Miguel. Thank you for seeing us."

"Jane is family here. It's nice to meet you. Sarah and Jane filled us in. You think you can stop this?"

"We'll need a lot of help and even more luck." Hali turned and introduced the rest of the team.

"Thank you for agreeing to meet with us," Jared said, his voice steady. Adam and Daniella stood beside him, the energy between them palpable.

"We think we can stop them," Jared continued, his eyes locked on Miguel's. "But a lot of things need to go right before that. We'll need more people and some of your knowledge of how to get around the AI so we aren't spotted and stopped before we even start."

"We aren't a militia. I can ask for volunteers, and we can share what we know that might help, but we're all about peace here. We've been painted in the media as some sort of bold and violent revolutionaries, but that isn't us. "

Before anyone could respond, the door flew open with a bang. Sarah burst into the room, her chest heaving as she fought for breath. "Mapenzie has disappeared!" she gasped. "Her latest anti-MedPal video went viral, and now she's gone!"

The room fell silent, except for Daniella's fingers tapping out a rapid beat on the table. Jared could see the concern etched on his team's faces, and they were all thinking the same thing: Mapenzie was in danger, and they were, too.

"Damn," Jared muttered under his breath. "She poked the bear, and it was only a matter of time before MedPal struck back. We must find her – and Motisha Sukoki – before it's too late."

"Sarah, do you have any leads on Mapenzie's whereabouts?" Hali asked, trying to keep the worry from seeping into her voice.

"Nothing concrete," Sarah said, "But we've been monitoring chatter online. There are whispers that she might be in hiding somewhere. The louder voices say that she's been taken."

===

They stood in the center of the old Walmart in a meeting room. It has once been the employee lounge. An old-fashioned movie theater popcorn machine lurked in the corner, spilling the aroma of buttered popcorn. Mismatched chairs, couches, and even a hammock were scattered across the room. A couple of empty vending machines lined the wall, their glass faces open hungrily like baby birds waiting to be fed.

Miguel walked into the room. "I've got some volunteers."

Men and women streamed into the room. They were an interesting mix. Some were athletic, walking into the room like Olympians entering a competition. Others held tablets and holos, phones, and cords. They entered as if they were the A team, come to save the day. Their faces were grim and determined. A woman with short, auburn hair stepped forward. Tattoos covered her arms, shoulders, and neck. Her full sleeves told a story of a woman who wouldn't back down from a fight and wanted you to know it. She had a nose ring and pierced eyebrows. Her muscular body moved with the grace of a big cat. The orange-red highlights in her hair added to the illusion that she was as much a tiger as she was a woman. When she spoke, her voice was surprisingly light and musical.

"I'm Fresco." She said with a curt nod, then gestured to the men and women who had come in with her. "These are our best. We always thought a day might come when we'd have to fight for our choices. You seem to think that today might be that day. We're highly trained both in guerilla and cyber warfare. I trust these men and women with my life."

Her cool blue eyes turned to ice. She paused, her eyes finding and searching Hali's face. "I trust your sister. I know how much you sacrificed for her after your parents died. She says to trust you, so I do. Do you trust these people?" She tilted her head toward the side where Jared, Adam, and Daniella stood.

The room was thick with tension, everyone acutely aware of the formidable forces they were about to face. Would they be able to trust each other?

Hali nodded. The tension eased a bit.

Jared spoke. "It might not be today, but it will be soon. We're going to need to work on several fronts. We've got to find a way to help Mapenzie. We'll need to find a way to access the MedPal cloud, and we'll need to find Motisha Sukoki, if she even exists.

Fresco nodded at a woman who had plopped down on a bean bag chair, furiously swiping at her tablet. "Jenna can find anyone. She doesn't like to be touched and only speaks when she feels like it, but she can connect dots that other people can't even see. Give her some time."

They were taking on powerful adversaries, venturing into the unknown, searching for an enigmatic figure who held the key to their salvation. It was a daunting task, but one they faced head-on, bound by a shared purpose and a fierce determination to protect humanity from the evil that wanted to eradicate it. Was genocide even the right word for what the 144 was trying to do? Or would they need to add a new name to the dictionary: Planeticide?

===

Sarah threw down her tablet in frustration. She and several of her friends had been scouring social media for anything from Mapenzie. She had disappeared without a trace. Suddenly, she leaped up from the couch and shouted. "Jared! Jared, where are you?"

He pushed his way through the now crowded room. "What did you find?"

"Nothing-but she's got a MedPal, right? So can't you trace her through the MedPal?" She asked.

"Dammit, you're right! Why didn't I do that first?" Jared threw a kick of frustration to the nearby vending machine, closing it with a loud thunk. The entire room turned to him, but he was already deep in his tablet.

The room buzzed with activity. Someone had started the popcorn machine, and the smell of popcorn mixed with a deep, rich scent drifted through the room of coffee cups being filled and refilled.

===

Fresco gave a loud whistle, and the room quieted instantly. "What do we have so far?"

Jared cleared his throat, and it sounded like a growl in the quiet room. Everyone turned to look at him, and he stood up reluctantly. "I have some bad news. I've been unable to track Mapenzie's MedPal. That means she's no longer connected to it."

"No! You aren't saying she's dead?" Sarah blurted out what no one else wanted to say.

"That's not necessarily the only answer." He paused, reluctant to say what they were all thinking. "But it is the most likely one."

Jane moved to Sarah's side, hugging her tight as they burst into tears at the same time. Jenna moved over to Fresco and pointed to something on her tablet.

"We have something! Fresco called out. "I think Jenna has found Motisha." She held up the tablet. A pin was highlighted on the map. Daniella got there first and opened up the pin.

"Some of the most difficult terrain in the world." She noted. "It makes sense. No tech, challenging access. It's a perfect place to hide from the world. How would we get there? Shit, how did she get there?"

"We need 2500," Fresco said shortly.

"2500 what?"

Fresco jumped on a nearby chair and shouted. "Hey, Cuervo! Get your ass over here!"

As she shouted, a chorus of **Arriba! Abajo! Al-centro! Y-pa-dentro!** rang out in answer from the group. The non-Nawers looked at each other in puzzlement. It seemed an odd time to be doing shots.

A man detached himself from the crowd, the grin of a man who knew who he was showing a mouthful of pearly white teeth. He moved like a man in his twenties, but as he neared, they could see that he was closer to 60. He was small-almost eye to eye with Daniella's five feet two inches, with wiry muscles and dusky skin.

"Yo Fresco. How can I help?" He spread his arms as if he were welcoming them to a party they weren't invited to. His gesture had an equal measure of welcome and warning. On one arm, a marijuana leaf appeared to be smoldering as the tattooed smoke curled upwards. On the other arm, a small bottle of Cuervo 2500 tequila seemed to be pouring itself into a shot glass. A lime wedge and a salt shaker were inked below the glass.

Fresco grinned back. "Cuervo, meet your team. I think they want to play with some of your toys."

She turned to Jared and the others. "Cuervo seems to be impervious to alcohol. He can drink men three times his size under the table and still walk a straight line. He's our chief engineer, gadget guy, and party planner all rolled up in one. Don't underestimate him, and don't ever party with him unless you want to wake up naked in public places."

Daniella raised one eyebrow. She scanned him from head to toe, a ghost of a smile on her face. "We need a miracle. Do you have one?"

===

The morning sun filtered through the blinds, casting stripes of light across Jared's face. He blinked awake, pulling Emma close to him. She murmured softly as she turned towards him. They made love softly, slowly, each savoring the familiar sensations as they brought each other pleasure. They delayed their gratification as long as they could, knowing that this might be the last time they were together for a while, and maybe forever.

"Jane says I have to go soon. She's moving all of us around frequently. She doesn't want to risk that they may have infiltrated us, and we'll be recognized." Emma gazed up at the man she had loved her entire adult life, her lithe fingers bringing his head down for one last kiss. "You have to come back to me. Promise?"

"Promise." He replied. It was a promise he might not be able to keep.

They dressed quickly, determined they would find their way back to each other.

123

Chapter 9: Search

They gathered again at the community center. Someone had come in overnight and cleaned up, but the room still smelled of popcorn and coffee.

Fresco spoke up. "Jenna got us a general location. Now, we have to try to narrow it down. We need to know every rumor, gossip, or fairy tale that has ever been spoken about Motisha to get closer. I'm not sending valuable resources unless we can have something more."

The room got quiet again as they each found a place to work. Daniella and Adam sat together at a table, their silence filled with unspoken feelings.

===

Sarah stared at her screen, her mouth falling open in horror. She had opened an alert, and her screen began to autoplay the latest Mapenzie video. But it wasn't Mapenzie. Her signature long box braids and striking figure were unmistakable, but something was off. Mapenzie's face was expressionless, her eyes vacant as she began to tout the benefits of MedPal. But at least she was alive. Or was she?

"Guys! Get over here!" Sarah called out, her voice trembling. She cast the video onto the big screen.

"Isn't that...?" Fresco began, her words trailing off.

"Mapenzie," Daniella whispered, clenching her fists in a mix of fear and anger. "And she's singing the praises of MedPal again. But look how strange. She has no expressions or animation. She looks like a robot."

"Or a puppet," Hali added, narrowing her eyes at the screen. "This isn't her at all. At least we know she's alive."

"Is she? Or did they just make a bot of her?" Sarah said bitterly. "Why wouldn't they just do an impers? "

"Impers?" Jane asked.

"Impersonation. If they can make Michael Jackson live, they can make Mapenzie say whatever they want."

"It's a warning. They want us to know what they're capable of." Daniella said. "They think they're unstoppable and want us to be afraid."

"MedPal is your ultimate companion for all medical needs," Mapenzie droned monotonously, her magnetic presence reduced to nothing more than an empty shell. "Trust in MedPal for a healthier tomorrow."

Sarah bit her lip, trying to contain the surge of emotions as she watched her friend being used as a pawn in this twisted game. She glanced around at her teammates, each wearing a mix of determination and concern. They had to find a way to help Mapenzie, and fast.

"I think she's alive, and there has to be something we can do," Sarah said, her voice firm and resolute. "Right, Hali? " Her eyes implored her sister to agree.

Hali hesitated. "It depends on what they've done to her. But yes, it seems she's alive, and that means we should have hope."

The team nodded in agreement, their eyes locked on the screen displaying the eerie image of their beloved friend, now a mere tool for those behind the scenes. "Her followers are going to know something's up," Adam said.

"Or they're going to be confused as hell and think that this is just some joker doing an off-ware spoof for practice," Fresco replied. "Either way, her followers aren't going to believe what she's saying. They did it to warn us and to create doubt of her credibility. And maybe they aren't ready to draw attention to themselves by hacking the anti-impers on her vids. They could do it, but that would trigger an Accord report unless they've figured a way around it."

==

"Wait, look at her wrist," Daniella exclaimed, pointing at the screen. "That's not the MedPal that we hacked to turn off when she left. She had the silver model. They only come in silver, gold, black, or white. That one isn't standard. It looks more like bronze than gold."

"Good catch, Hali," Jared praised, his dark eyes narrowing as he studied the image more closely. "Whatever that device is, it's not a standard MedPal.

We need to figure out how they control her through that device."

"And we need to get it off her!" Sarah added.

"Stay strong, Mapenzie," Sarah whispered as she renewed her efforts to find a way to enter the city without being discovered. Her fiery orange hair reflected the burning determination in her eyes. "We're coming for you."

===

I don't think they've killed her. She's compliant, robotic, and devoid of her usual indomitable spirit. There are some for whom a sexbot won't be enough. They'll want a real person to humiliate. Weak men need to feel powerful, and what would make them feel more powerful than being able to take away free will? It's next-level slavery. "

"Technology has always been used to oppress the masses, especially women," Daniella interjected passionately. "From the days when reading and writing was only available to the privileged few, all the way to what they're doing now with MedPal."

"True," Hali agreed, nodding solemnly. "And Mapenzie was a symbol of resistance to that oppressive system. She built her entire career on empowering people and giving them a voice using AI."

"Which makes her the perfect target for them," Adam added. "They want to turn her into a puppet and use her influence to further their own twisted agenda."

"Right," Sarah agreed, clenching her fists in resolve. "Let's get Mapenzie back and show these bastards that they can't control us."

They pressed on despite the exhaustion that bore down on them. They powered through with countless cups of coffee and energy drinks, refusing to let themselves be defeated by fatigue. Jared's fingers danced across his tablet while Hali pored over medical reports. Sarah and Jane scoured the web for any information on mind control technology, and Adam used his vast resources to search for connections between the 144 and MedPal.

The room was a cacophony of determined whispers, furious typing, and frantic screen swiping as everyone worked in unison toward their ultimate goal: saving Mapenzie and bringing the truth to light.

Just as spirits began waning, Adam burst into the room, triumphantly holding up a tablet. "I've got it!" he exclaimed, his face alight with excitement. "A lead on Motisha! I believe I can show you where she's hiding out."

"How?" Daniella asked

"I used a search bot and found a reference to *Ophiocordyceps unilateralis.* The zombie ant?" He looked at their confused faces and explained. "There is this mushroom that turns ants into zombies. It's part of the reproductive cycle of the mushroom. There aren't that many places where it lives. She mentioned it in her release of the code. Something about how AI could turn us into zombie ants if we didn't use it carefully. Then I found another reference attributed to her where she is said to have likened the diversity of humanity to the diversity of plant life. She posited that AI needed to be trained by natural systems to understand interdependency and never see any part of the system as bad or unnecessary."

He paused to take a breath. "Man! What a mind she has! Anyway, only one place on Earth has zombie ants **and** the most diversity of life on the planet. Jenna was right. She's deep in the Amazon, and I think she's where the Amazon meets the Andes mountains."

"One of the most inaccessible places on the planet. We have no way of getting there!" Jared said grimly.

"Leave that to me," Cuervo replied. He walked out the door, beckoning them to follow.

===

The barn still had an old *Chew Mail Pouch Tobacco* ad on the warped boards. The doors hung on their hinges, and an old tarp covered the doorway. The roof was partially sunken on one side, and the old boards were so weathered it was impossible to tell what color they might have been.

Cuervo beamed with pride as he swept open the tarp to reveal a second set of doors. They were solid and secured with several complicated locks. When he finally stepped aside and waved them in, This was no abandoned barn. High-tech equipment was strewn across workbenches, and the metal bones of what might have been the start of a robot stood about eight feet high in the corner.

"What the fuck is that??" Adams eyes swept the cluttered space and landed on an old, wooden biplane that dominated the back of the 'barn. "Please tell me that isn't your plan."

Jared chimed in. "That thing looks like it flew at Kitty Hawk. Did you steal it from a museum?"

Cuervo just chuckled. "Dudes, you have no idea. This is a de Havilland Dragon Rapide. She is a jewel of aviation. State of the art for her time; she was one of the first private jets. A 1930s short-haul biplane airliner. Isn't she beautiful?" Cuervo asked, running his hand lovingly along the sleek fuselage. "She may look old-fashioned, but she's packing some cutting-edge tech under the hood."

"Is that really plywood?" Emma asked, rapping her knuckles on the side of the plane.

"Well, I wanted to keep her like the original, at least as much as possible. Respect, you know. That's a nanocomposite magnesium alloy made to seem like plywood. When I started, this baby was equipped with Gipsy Six engines, tapered wings, and streamlined fairings. It broke my heart to have to make some minor tweaks, but you gotta move with the music, and she needed something more than what she had." He gestured vaguely to a nearby pile of metal partially covered by a tarp.

"Someday, I'm gonna put her back together again the way she originally was. For now, though, she has turbofan engines, aerogels for insulation, wing morphing capabilities, and can take you across the globe in hours."

He turned and swept his arms under the plane as if he were revealing a masterpiece. "TA DA! The pièce de resistance... 'blinders.' " He looked at them expectantly as if waiting for applause. When they didn't react, he explained. "It's a system that emits wavelengths of sound and light, making her invisible to modern tracking systems."

"Brilliant!" Adam exclaimed. "When we have time, I want to hear the story of how you got all that tech. Most of it was still experimental last time I heard."

Cuervo nodded and winked. "Yeah, well, I do love me a 'speriment'."

"Now all we have to do is figure out who's going," Jared said.

"Count me in," Sarah declared without hesitation.

Cuervo interrupted. "She can carry eight- nine if she has to, but that includes pilot and copilot. So, you got me and Amy. If you count this Motisha, you got one coming back, but what if she has peeps, too? Muscle is a good idea where we're goin' - we should take Mac. Just two of you, I think. If we don't find lady mysterious, we need people back here workin' on the other stuff."

"Alright," Adam conceded, tugging on his beard. "Daniella, you can come with us. You know the most about Motisha. You're also the one most likely to understand the tech. We can't bet it all on this long shot, so we need people here working on getting into the MedPal cloud."

Daniella raised an eyebrow. "I CAN come with you? You're giving me permission? How thoughtful," she said dryly. "Little ole me is just *thrilled* to have your permission. I think all that mess on your face is your brain coming out of your face."

"Dani, come on, I didn't mean it that way." Adam implored. "We need you."

"Damn right you do. As long as you remember that having a penis doesn't mean you're in charge." She turned away from him.

Sarah interrupted. "And we need to try to save Mackenzie. She just posted another video, and her followers can see something is wrong. It could put her in even more danger if they keep agitating."

The team stood silently for a moment, staring at the seemingly old biplane. Jane took a deep breath. "Cuervo, I know you're the best. Just don't take any unnecessary risks."

He grinned and winked. "I'll be back, Mamacita. I have plans for us." He wiggled his hips obscenely, making everyone laugh except Jane, who blushed a deep, dusky red. He looked at something on his tablet, then turned to the others. "Our best takeoff window is in 30 minutes, so we need to move."

Twenty minutes later, they stood looking at the plane once more. Daniella touched the side of the plane. "It sure feels like plywood. I guess if we survive this, I'll be over my fear of flying."

"I got you, Amiga," Cuervo said with confidence. "Here's the rest of the team.

"Let me introduce you to your copilot. This is Amy," Cuervo said as he opened the plane door. Sitting in the co-pilot seat was an athletic woman with a long dark braid down her back. She exuded an air of calm confidence as she smiled at them,

"Fasten your seat belts, folks. You're in for the ride of your life." Amy joked. Daniella looked queasy. "We have barf bags, so you'll be fine. I hope you didn't eat too much garlic. Smells up the whole plane when it comes back up."

"She's joking," Cuervo assured them. "And here comes Mac."

Striding towards them was a bald man wearing cargo pants and a tight black t-shirt. He was big- 6'3" of solid muscle. The leather suspenders he wore looked incongruous until you noticed the sheaths attached up and down each one, knives within easy reach.

He came at them like a freight train, a thunderous glare in his eyes. He flicked his wrist, and a knife appeared in his hand. "My real name's Francis, but if you call me that, you'll meet one of my knives up close and personal." His smile said he was joking- maybe. Another flick, and the knife was gone.

"Fair enough," Daniella said, eyeing the weapons warily. "Mac it is."

"Jesus, we're like that fuckin' asteroid movie where they pull together a ragtag group of strangers and tell them to save the world," Adam said.

"Then let's go blow up an asteroid."

===

Everyone stopped as the boom of the jet hitting sonic speed was heard in the distance. Jane said a silent prayer, then turned to Sarah.

"Nobody's better than Cuervo. If it can be done, he'll do it. Come on, we have work to do." She turned and walked towards an old grain silo. "It's getting crowded at the community hall, and Jared and Hali wanted a quieter place to work."

Chapter 10: Found

Hali sipped her lukewarm tea, trying to find the right words. Sarah sat by the window with a furrowed brow and uneasy expression. It looked like she'd put on someone else's face. The smile was gone, the sparkle muted. Had Hali caused this? Was she too hard on her little sister?

"Sarah, I need to apologize," Hali began. "I was wrong to underestimate the life you were living. I've treated you like you were still the skinny twelve-year-old that I used to help with her homework. You have become such an amazing woman. Your work with the Nawers has given us valuable contacts, and I should've acknowledged that sooner."

A slight smile tugged at the corner of Sarah's mouth, but it didn't reach her eyes. She looked away. "Thanks, but we're both just doing our part. Besides, it's all about the Twinkies."

Hali studied her sister's face, noting the tightness around her eyes and how she avoided eye contact. Something was off. "Is everything all right?" she asked. Not even the joke about Twinkies had eased the tightness in her sister's voice.

"Of course," Sarah replied too quickly, her gaze darting back to meet Hali's. "It's just... I'm worried about Mapenzie. What if it isn't reversible? What if they've done something permanent to her?"

Hali nodded, recalling the charismatic influencer's recent broadcasts. Any trace of Mapenzie in the voice or mannerisms was gone. She was nothing but a speaking mannequin. It was eerie to watch.

Brain plasticity can overcome severe damage. There are reasons for hope. It's not in your nature to be a pessimist, Sarah. Is something else bothering you? What is it? "

Sarah hesitated, and Hali could see the internal struggle playing out behind her eyes. Finally, she sighed and shook her head. "No, it's just Mapenzie. And everything. I promise."

"Okay," Hali relented, though the unease in her gut remained. She forced a smile and took another sip of her tea, trying to push aside the nagging sense that her sister was hiding something. If Sarah wanted to talk, she would.

===

Hali knocked on the door. "Sarah? Do you want some lunch? I haven't seen you since breakfast." She knocked again, then turned the knob and peeked in. Sarah wasn't there, and there was a note on her bed.

"Please don't be mad, sis. This is something that only I can do. I love you all, and I'll be back. No matter what happens, trust me."

Hali's heart clenched with worry as she clutched the note, her mind racing with questions. What had Sarah gotten herself into? Was it related to Mapenzie or something else entirely? She reread the note, hoping that somehow more words would appear or that she had read it wrong. The words remained the same.

===

Jane shook her head as she read the note that Hali had passed her. "I have no idea where she went. That girl has always had secrets. The perimeter alerts didn't go off, but I wouldn't be surprised if she knew a way to get around them."

Jane patted Hali's pale cheek. "Hush, child. I know you think she's still a little girl, but Sarah has been a grown woman for a long time and has smarts and skills. We have to do what she asked and trust her."

Hali nodded reluctantly. They had no choice.

===

Jared paced the silo, his footsteps echoing in as he paced. "Shouldn't we have heard from them by now?"

Fresco looked up from the search code she was writing. "Cuervo is the best. It's only been two days. You need to relax." She stood up, stretching her back, then spun around, looking up. "Check this place out. This was a fucking grain silo. Given the strength of the jammers all over this place, we've got access to tools and information that should be impossible. The dude could make you a fucking rocket from the shit he found in a dumpster. He's not going to risk communication until he has to. He's doing his job-we need to do ours."

Jared looked around. She was right. The silo loomed over them, and near the top were satellite dishes, wires, and something like a sixty's era tv antennae. Screens were scattered about in various stages of repair. Some were open in the back, fresh soldering gleaming in the light. Strewn throughout the silo, things that were cobbled together were made better. Even the air fryer oven had been modified and was now a cross between a microwave, a pressure cooker, and an air fryer. Yet, with all the merryrigging, things here were more reliable than they had been in his ultra-modern office.

Jared nodded. "You're right. This place is amazing. It just seems like we're up against impossible odds."

Fresco barked a laugh, shaking her head. "Shit, impossible odds are great compared to some of the odds we've overcome. Jane kept people alive during the Crush with fucking herbal tea and mustard packs. While people were starving, we were eating shit I'd never seen before, but we thrived. We ate weeds and shrooms and lizard eggs, and I don't know what the fuck else. I didn't want to know. When people were freezing to death, we were warm as piss and building networks that connected Nawer communities everywhere. Nawers were fucking awesome before you Kool-Aid-drinking AI-ers even knew that shit was gonna come down hard. Nawers saw it coming long before you gave us a name. You call us the Nawers because you think we said no to some of the tech. We didn't say no to tech. We said no to putting shit in our bodies and in control of our world before the capabilities and dangers were understood. We learned from history. People have been saying shit is good when it's deadly just to make a buck since the beginning of time."

She paused. "I get it, Mr. 'I-make-a-fortune-on-tech.' You've never really seen poverty and what happens to people. They always sell bad shit to people who are trapped in poverty. Cigs, vapes, cheap booze, cheap entertainment, and just enough hope to keep them on the hamster wheel. You didn't have lead in your water, chemicals that caused cancer and birth defects in your yard, and food that guaranteed that you'd stay sick, stupid, and small. And I bet you donated to food banks and charities with nice names like Homes for Humanity and Food for All. You saw yourself as a fine human being, doing your part while you consumed ten times the resources of anyone else, and felt great when you gave a big tip to your server or dropped a twenty in a homeless person's cup. You call us Nawers as an insult. We wear it with pride, 'cause to us it means we said 'Naw' to your fucked up patriarch greedy shit." She turned back to her work, not even bothering to see his reaction.

Jared opened his mouth to protest, to refute what she had said, then closed it again. There was too much truth in what she said.

===

Jane and Hali sat around a table, the cool evening air drifting through the window. A quick knock, and the door handle turned. "It's open," Jane said as Emma walked into the room. "I had to come back. I know Jared sent me away to protect me, but I need to be useful. If we don't stop this, they'll come for us. Maybe we can run or hide for a while- a few years. But eventually, they'll find us." Emma looked at Jane. "But

I'm glad that we found you. Even if we don't make it, this time has been the best of my life. I feel strangely hopeful despite there being no cause for hope."

Jane nodded. "Community, nature, and resilience. It's what has kept humans going for millennia. No matter what kind of world it is – whether running from the tiger or running from the corruption that has always been part of our world- cooperation, community, and cultivating individual skills so that each member of the community is living their highest expression- that's what makes life have meaning. It is always a time to be hopeful."

"Sarah," Hali whispered, hearing Jane's words. "Be strong. Come back to us."

Jane reached out and squeezed her hand, a hundred tomes of unspoken words in the gesture.

"Trust me," the note had said. Hali clung to those words like a lifeline, praying that Sarah would find her way back to them wherever she was.

===

Jane and Hali awoke to a soft but persistent knocking in the early morning hours.

A man stood in the dim moonlight. A taller figure was leaning heavily on his shoulder. Jane quickly recognized the man from one of the neighboring communities.

"Jasper?" Jane asked, then gasped when she recognized the figure he was supporting. "Mapenzie! Oh, thank Gaia!" She grabbed Mapenzie's arm and helped him bring her inside. She fell heavily onto the floral couch, her head lolling to one side.

The once-vibrant influencer was nearly unrecognizable. Her long box braids were disheveled, and her usually magnetic presence was replaced by a hollow emptiness.

"Mapenzie," Hali gasped, rushing forward to examine her. "How did you escape?"

Jared answered. "We found her on the perimeter. We tried to remove her MedPal, but she screamed so loud we stopped. He explained, his voice grim. "We needed to act fast because there's more at stake here than just her health."

"Of course," Hali answered, her physician instincts taking over. She assessed Mapenzie's condition, her gentle hands steadying the trembling woman. Jane went to make tea. For Jane, tea was the answer to everything.

"Let's get her stable first," Hali decided, her voice firm but calm. "Then we can figure out what to do next."

"She showed up a few hours ago. The boundary alert was triggered, and when we got there, she was sitting against a tree, and someone was running away. As long as that thing is on her wrist, we're all in danger."

Mapenzie was struggling to say something. Hali leaned in close. "Shhhh. You need to rest."

"Sssarahhh. Mapenzie's voice was barely audible as she struggled to speak. "T-t-traitor."

Hali recoiled. Was Mapenzie saying that Sarah was a traitor? It was impossible. No one else had heard it, so she just shook her head when Jane and Jasper looked at her quizzically.

"I have to get back," Jasper said grimly. "We don't know if she's led trouble to our door. We're on high alert, and I suggest you do the same."

Hours later, as the first light of dawn began to paint the sky, Hali's and Jane's phones buzzed simultaneously. The message to both was identical. And short. Her heart skipped a beat when she read the short but alarming text:

"Get everyone out – now! It's TWINKIE TIME!"

Hali's hands trembled as she read the message again, trying to understand what it meant. Jane, looking equally rattled, met Hali's gaze.

"It's got to be from Sarah. Right?"

"Maybe," Jane said, her brow furrowed with worry. "But we don't know if this isn't someone trying to flush us out. Sarah's Twinkie addiction is well known."

Hali nodded, her mind racing with thoughts and questions. Was Sarah in danger? Had they been infiltrated? And what did Mapenzie mean? Was she calling Sarah a traitor or saying that Sarah was betrayed? In her heart, Hali could only believe the latter. Sarah would never betray them.

===

The Nawers gathered quickly, the silo filling up in a matter of minutes. As soon as Jane had outlined the situation, Fresco spoke up. "The shelters. Ten people stepped forward.

"What shelters?" Jane asked, her confusion mirrored on many other faces around her.

"You always believed in the best outcomes, Jane," Fresco said. "You know the saying, hope for the best, plan for the worst. You did the hope thing. We did the plan thing. There's an underground complex about half a mile away. We have a lot of bunker freaks in our communities. There are hidey holes all over the place. For us, it's some old military shit abandoned and forgotten, probably in the 70s. Miguel encouraged all the communities to have bugout shelters and plans for evacuation if things got dicey. This is ours. The team leaders know what to do." She gestured at the ten who had stepped forward. "Evacuate."

It took less than five minutes for them to organize everyone into groups. The strongest helped Mapenzie and an elderly woman who couldn't keep up. As they hurried forward in the breaking dawn, the distant hum of drones broke the morning stillness.

===

Hali's heart raced as she glanced at the sky, scanning for the ominous drones. The sound grew louder, a chilling reminder of the power that loomed over them all.

"Keep moving!" Fresco shouted, her voice encouraging yet firm. It was clear that while Jane was the one they turned to in the times of peace, Fresco was the woman to follow now.

The team leaders guided their groups swiftly into the hidden entrance, disappearing into the darkness below. Hali took one last look around her and followed suit, the weight of Sarah's absence hanging heavy on her mind. She knew they were fighting against time, and every second mattered.

Once inside, the air was cool, a stark contrast to the warmth of the morning sun outside. Jane stood at the entrance, her mouth hanging open as she looked around. "What is the place? Fresco, why didn't I know about this?"

Fresco's reply was short and to the point. "Need to know. Less ears that hear, less mouths to talk."

As they moved deeper into the complex, the sound of the drones above gradually faded. Fresco led them through a series of winding tunnels before stopping in a square chamber that had clearly been an old command center. It was here that they would regroup and plan their next move. But for now, they needed to catch their breath and assess their situation.

One of the team leaders walked over to a screen and pushed a button. The screen came alive with scenes from all over their community. Drones were everywhere. About ten of them had landed and switched to land mode, looking like giant metal beetles scurrying over the landscape.

"Give me sound!" Fresco barked. The person at the console pushed a button, and the insect-like hum of drones echoed off the walls. Several massive autonomous Humvees screeched to a halt by the community dining area, and armed soldiers poured out.

"Peacekeeping forces my ass," muttered Fresco.

The leader was unmistakable. It wasn't just his military bearing. He exploded out of the first vehicle, his long strides taking him to the community hall door and through it in seconds. The bang of the door hitting the wall sounded like a gunshot.

He walked away from the empty building, fury on his face. He screamed into the face of a young man standing defiantly by the door. "She said they'd be here! If your girl is lying, there will be hell to pay, and you and she will be the ones to pay it. I don't give a flying fuck who your father is. We need to shut these people down, and we need to do it now."

The young man locked eyes with him, his face a mask. "Dude, I just got some from the girl. I hardly know her." He turned away, his body language echoing the insolence in his tone.

"Search everywhere!" The leader yelled in fury. Spittle sprayed from his mouth as he screamed.

Hali's heart raced as she watched the scene unfold on the screen. She could feel the tension in the room, everyone on edge, wondering if they would be discovered. Jane gripped Hali's arm tightly, her knuckles turning white.

Chapter 11: Motisha

Cuervo's steady hands gripped the controls of the aircraft, his eyes darting between the instrument panel and the dense foliage rapidly approaching. The silence was thick with anticipation as each considered the magnitude of the task ahead.

The inside of the plane was a bizarre mix of antique and high-tech. The emergency exit was a hatch in the roof of the plane. It was as low-tech as you could get, with a metal lever that had to be operated manually. The cockpit was a complicated array of displays, gauges, and levers that Cuervo and Amy worked like virtuosos.

"Amigas and Amigos, strap yourself in. I think I found a place to take us in." His jovial voice could be heard above the roar of the engines.

"Jesus Cuervo-there's nothing down there but a jungle. Where the fuck do you see a place to land a plane?" Adams's head swiveled from window to window, looking for a place open enough to land a plane.

Before Cuervo could answer, the plane shuddered and began to plunge and buck. A downdraft sent them towards the mountainside, and Cuervo and Amy's fingers flew over buttons and dials. Alarms blared, drowning out the panicked thoughts that raced through everyone's minds. Cuervo fought the stick like it was a bronco, and he was determined to tame it.

"Cuervo, what's happening?" Daniella cried out, her voice straining to be heard above the cacophony.

"Wind shear!" he shouted back, struggling to keep the plane steady. "Hang on!"

As the aircraft bucked violently, Daniella grabbed onto Adam. Her face was white with fear. He didn't hesitate; he just wrapped his arms around her, pulling her tight against his solid frame. "I got you, Dani. I got you. Breathe. You're okay." His voice soothed her as the plane was yanked up and then down as if some giant hand was using it as a yo-yo.

"Adam," she spoke urgently, her breath hot against his ear, "I'm sorry I left you like that. I thought our ideological differences would make it impossible, and I was stubborn and sure I was right about it all. Now it seems so unimportant."

Her words hung heavy in the chaos, but Adam didn't hesitate. He tightened his embrace, silently reassuring her as the world threatened to tear apart around them.

Through sheer force of will and skill, Cuervo managed to regain control of the aircraft. The alarms ceased their shrill warnings, replaced by the collective sighs of relief from the team.

As the danger passed, Danielle began to pull away. He pulled her closer. "Dani, none of it matters now. We're in this together, and I'll always be here for you. No matter what. Even if it did take a near-death experience for you to finally admit that you can't live without me," he ended jokingly.

He looked into her eyes; his face full of longing. "I never stopped loving you, you know."

Mac's voice cut through the relief. "Damn, Cuervo. You could have warned me that I'd need an extra set of underwear. I do believe I might have shat myself."

"Just like you did in '29 when we hooked up with those sexbots you thought were real women and tried to get them drunk by outdrinking them? Man, that was some funny shit!" His laughter filled the plane. Mac just grinned.

"Okay! Here we go!" Cuervo said with glee.

===

As the plane descended, the jungle canopy grew thicker. The team scanned the terrain below, their eyes darting between the intertwined branches and vines of the remote mountain jungle.

"I still don't see a place to land. Are you sure you aren't seeing things?" Adam's banter was underlined with tension.

Cuervo pointed at the spot, an opening in the trees that was about 30 feet across. The clearing was small and uneven, hardly an ideal place to set down the plane.

"There's no way," Adam yelled. That's not enough runway to land a hummingbird!"

Cuervo cackled with joy. "Watch this," he said as he pushed a button on the console.

The aircraft shifted abruptly, seeming to come to a dead stop in the air. The whir and whine of metal moving filled the cabin as the wings folded in. At the same time, something unfolded from the top. It began a vertical descent.

"Since when could it do that?" Mac asked.

"Always got a few tricks up my sleeve," Cuervo replied with a wink. "Now, let's get this bird down safely."

With precision and skill, Cuervo maneuvered the aircraft into the tight clearing, angling it vertically to accommodate for the rough terrain. They landed so lightly that it wasn't until Cuervo took his hands off the controls that the rest of the team realized they were down.

===

"Okay, the dragon has landed," Cuervo announced as he powered down the aircraft. "Don't forget to tip your pilots and copilots."

"Where are we?" Daniella asked, looking out the window at the dense foliage. Nobody answered her. It was only a GPS coordinate on a map.

"Remember to double-check your supplies," Adam reminded them. "We don't know what we'll encounter out there."

"Trust me, I'm more than prepared for whatever this jungle has in store for us," Mac said, patting his knives.

"Let's hope so," Daniella muttered under her breath, her fingers drumming nervously on her thigh.

The oppressive humidity hit them like a wall as they stepped out of the aircraft. The air was thick and heavy, making it difficult to breathe. They could feel the sweat beading on their foreheads almost immediately.

"Welcome to the jungle," Amy sang out in her best Axl Rose. Cuervo added in some air guitar.

"Nothing fazes you guys, does it?" Daniella asked a little jealously.

"Get your fun while you can, I always say!"

The cacophony of wildlife sounds enveloped them, wrapping around them like a living symphony. Birds cawed from high above, their calls echoing through the dense jungle. Insects buzzed incessantly, their drones nearly deafening. Somewhere far off, they heard the guttural growl of an unidentified creature, sending a shiver down their spines.

"Alright, let's move," Cuervo called, motioning the team to gather around him. "Stay alert and watch each other's backs. We don't know what surprises this jungle has in store for us."

"Or who might be waiting," Adam added, his voice low and serious.

The team nodded in agreement, their eyes scanning the shadows as they moved cautiously into the jungle. The ground was uneven and slick with moisture, making each step treacherous.

===

"Any idea where we're headed?" Mac asked, wiping the sweat from his brow as they trudged deeper into the jungle.

"That way," Cuervo joked, each hand pointed in a different direction. "If she's here, she'll probably find us. Keep moving, and let's make some noise." He began to sing in a loud, off-key voice.

"Oh fuck! Not the Happy Song. You promised." Mac complained

"*Because I'm happy!! Clap along if you know what happiness means to you.*" Cuervo's dance moves almost made up for his singing. Almost. He did an elaborate hand clap, spun around, and lightly punched Mac on the shoulder. "C'mon dude, you know you love it!"

Cuervo beamed and explained to the others. "Sang it for six hours straight when Mac got hit in the head, and I thought he had a concussion. Needed to keep his ass awake." He spun back around and did a little dance as they moved forward.

Everyone laughed and followed Mac and his machete as he chopped a path.

"Better than standing still," Daniella agreed, swatting away an enormous mosquito that had landed on her arm.

They walked on. Cuervo's terrible singing caused a flock of brilliant blue birds to fly up from the canopy, squawking in protest.

Mac slapped his ear as he felt a sharp sting on his earlobe, accompanied by the unmistakable sound of something whizzing past him. In an instant, he realized what had happened - a knife had just narrowly missed him, embedding itself into the tree trunk behind him.

"Down!" he shouted, grabbing the knife from the tree and quickly sliding behind the massive trunk.

Cuervo and Amy dove in opposite directions, hiding under the foliage.

Adam grabbed Daniella and pushed her to the ground, following immediately to cover her with his massive frame. Her heart pounded with fear.

There was a moment of tense silence before three more knives struck the tree, hitting almost simultaneously.

Fortunately, they had landed on a soft patch of ferns. Time stopped for a moment as he gazed into her eyes, the feeling of her beneath him bringing up so many memories.

Adam went to brush the hair from her eyes, and he froze. Coming towards them was the biggest, hairiest spider he'd ever seen. It was the size of a turkey platter. It stopped and made a skittering noise. He could see the massive fangs as it approached. It reminded him of the scene in the cave of the Harry Potter movie- the scene where he always closed his eyes.

The spider started to advance again as if it were stalking them. It was a tarantula on steroids, with a streak of red going down its back. His mind raced. Didn't bright colors mean it was poisonous? Jesus, what should he do?

Daniella squirmed underneath him, trying to see what he was seeing. He couldn't let her see it. They were both arachnophobes. They called him Spider-Man in college because he called the RA to kill a spider in his bathroom. A few well-played football tackles during pickup games had ended the nickname but not the terror he felt when he saw a spider.

His heart pounded with fear. His greatest nightmare was here, and the woman he had loved for so long was in danger. He couldn't lose her again. He had to man up and fast.

The spider was less than a foot away. It was already crawling on her hair, and she was still trying to turn her head to see what he was looking at.

She squirmed beneath him, trying to see what he saw. The terror he was feeling melded with the response his body was making to her wild gyrations. Much later, he would realize he was no longer afraid of spiders; instead, they made him weirdly horny.

He had no choice. At the same moment he bent his head to kiss her, he flung his arm out, sending the spider flying. He didn't know if he'd been bitten or not, but he knew that if this were the way he would die, it wasn't the worst way to go. He forgot about the spider and got lost in the kiss.

Cuervo glanced at Mac and gestured toward the direction the knives had come from, indicating that he would try to circle around and find the source. Cuervo began to move through the underbrush silently. The team remained hidden, their nerves stretched tight except Daniella and Adam. The kiss absorbed them, and the years melted away.

===

Cuervo had almost completed his crawl when a booming laugh filled the jungle, echoing from every direction. "C'mon Mon," the voice called out in a heavy Jamaican accent, targeting Mac. "Are those little pins on your chest just for show? I'm dead wid laugh at the look on your face. Here I be thinking you come to play, but you be hidin' in the trees like a gyal!"

Mac's jaw clenched, but he remained still, knowing that revealing their position could endanger the entire team.

Another voice chimed in, seemingly coming from everywhere and nowhere at once. "Ah, Gwin wit ya Tacky. Stop ur foolin' and show them the way." The same voice continued, without the accent. "Don't mind Tacky. He likes a bit of fun. I've been expecting you. Hi Dani! It's been a while. I thought you'd figure it out sooner."

Adam and Dani jumped to their feet, brushing the jungle floor from their clothes.

"I know that voice!" She declared. "But it can't be. You're dead."

"Do I sound dead?" The voice came back, filled with amusement.

"Jennifer Chin! It can't be!"

"But it is."

'You're Motisha? Of course you are! You were, I mean are, the smartest woman ever to walk the earth. I cried for months when you died! How could you do that to us? And to your mom!" The words came tumbling out, unstoppable.

"Do you want to keep yelling at me, or would you rather get out of the jungle before a snake wraps around your neck- or a spider falls on your head?"

Daniella grabbed the top of her head with a shriek. There was nothing there. "I'll wait until I see you to yell some more. Get us out of here!"

"Patience, gyal," Tacky's voice rang out again, this time accompanied by the rustling of leaves as a tall man with dreadlocks emerged from the shadows, grinning broadly. His massive frame dwarfed even Mac, and the machetes slung across his back were razor-sharp. "We ave sum walkin' tuh duh before wi get innna whulla dat."

Exchanging wary glances, the team followed him as he swung the machete with practiced ease.

===

They stopped by a thicket of vines and brambles. They'd only been walking a short while. The thicket had evil-looking spikes at least an inch long, and a flower lazily opened up to reveal sharp teeth and a sticky interior. "Little shop of horrors," Amy commented, referencing the cult classic.

Tacky turned abruptly, his dreadlocks whipping like snakes. The jovial facade was gone, and a menacing glower had replaced it. When he spoke, the Jamaican accent was gone.

"She trusts you." He pointed to Daniella. "I trust no one."

His eyes drilled into each one of them for a moment, the silence heavy. Finally, he nodded. "Your plane scanned clean, and so did all of you. One wrong move, and you'll be bleeding before you can take your next breath." He nodded pointedly at Mac.

"Understood," Cuervo replied, his voice steady despite the tension. The others nodded in agreement, understanding that Tacky's warning was not to be taken lightly.

"Good," Tacky said, and his Jamaican accent returned as he flashed a grin. "Now, mek wi gwan." With that, he tilted his head, flicked his fingers over several spikes in a row in a pattern too quick for them to follow, and stepped back.

The thicket parted like the Red Sea. Tacky's broad shoulders brushed the spikes as they walked single file toward a cliff that rose before them.

Chapter 12: Betrayed?

The air in the makeshift conference room was thick with tension, a palpable unease that seemed to seep into every corner. The team was gathered around a hastily assembled group of tables, brows furrowed and gazes darting between one another.

Jared leaned against the wall, his arms crossed as he studied the faces of his friends and colleagues, all of them on edge. "Nobody wants to say it, but it has to be said. Isn't it a little suspicious that Sarah disappeared, and we're suddenly compromised? "

A drone buzzed loudly on the screens as it circled the compound. Its ominous hum was a relentless reminder of their situation. The community was being watched constantly by eyes that never blinked. The drones circled overhead like vultures, waiting for the moment to swoop in and pick at the remains of their shattered trust.

"Couldn't they have also put a tracker on Mapenzie?" Fresco muttered, her fingers running through her short red hair. "We've got to assume they know everything about us." She paused. "We've warned the other communities. A global alert has gone out. They won't find anything anywhere. Everyone has evacuated the known communities. So there's that. But they can trap us here forever if we don't find a way out that isn't going to be seen by the drones."

"What about another exit?" Emma asked. "Have you explored the whole area down here?"

"We were too busy ensuring we had what we needed in case of..." She waved her hands at the screen that was showing several drones doing a grid search over the compound. "...that."

Jared clenched his fists, "Maybe Sarah betrayed us. Maybe she didn't. It doesn't matter right now."

"It sure as hell does! Sarah wouldn't betray us. She's one of us. I don't think someone who works for Eos has the right to suggest that she would!" The uncharacteristic anger in Janes' voice brought the room to silence. The drones continued their relentless patrol outside, their ceaseless hum a constant reminder that time was running out.

Miguel broke the silence. "I don't believe Sarah betrayed us. I do believe that we need to work together. If you're in this bunker, you're a Nawer unless you prove us wrong. We don't do the us and them shit here. Hali and Jared, figure out how to get that MedPal off of Mapenzie and see if you can find out if they're tracking her."

"She didn't betray us," Jane replied, crossing her arms defiantly. "There has to be an explanation. I've known that child since she was still in her Mama's belly. There's something here that we don't know. They forced her somehow or manipulated her. It's the only explanation."

"Let's focus on what we can do. You heard Miguel. We're all us in this place, and right now, a powerful them is looking to fuck us up. So pair up and explore unless you're running a screen or unable to. I want to know what our resources are."

They slowly drifted off, their footsteps echoing through the darkened tunnel as they ventured deeper into the gloom. Jane walked down a side tunnel with her good friend. Adriana. Her mind raced as she swept her flashlight over the grey walls, searching for any sign of an exit. She understood the others' suspicions but couldn't believe Sarah would betray them. "Not in a million years," She whispered to herself.

As the teams moved through the labyrinthine network of tunnels, their voices crackled over the comms, sharing updates and discoveries. They found remnants of old living quarters, abandoned storage rooms, and an old, rusted-out gasoline-run generator. The tunnels seemed to go on forever, randomly branching off in strange places, with dead ends and places that looked like someone had stopped mid-construction.

===

Hali and Jared went to the room where Mapenzie was lying down. She was unresponsive. "Her vitals are stable. I'm not sure why she's unresponsive. Can you scan the device and see if there are any malfunctions?" Hali asked.

"I don't understand it. I'm showing two programs running simultaneously. That shouldn't even be possible. There is a lot of brain activity, considering she's unresponsive. I think we need to try to remove it."

Mapenzie's eyes began moving rapidly beneath her eyelids. She murmured something. "What did she say?" Hali asked.

"I didn't hear it."

Mapenzie began singing. "*I'm every woman; it's all in me.*" Hali and Jared looked at each other in puzzlement. Why was she singing Whitney Houston? Why was she singing at all?

The song changed. "*I am woman; hear me roar in numbers too big to ignore.*"

They stepped away. Mapenzie kept singing. It was a montage of female empowerment songs, but her eyes were closed, and she didn't respond to their attempts to talk to her.

"Is there anything you can think of that can explain this?" Hali asked.

"No. It's bizarre. Let's try to remove the device."

"She's got a great voice. I'll monitor her vitals while you remove it."

Mapenzie's eyes flew open when Jared attempted to release the clasp. "Don't. It's helping me."

Jared looked at his screen. "One of the programs is now dominant. Mapenzie, we need to know what is going on. Can you help us understand? Do you know what's happening to you?"

While he was speaking, she was humming Janelle Monae's *Americans.*

"It's learning about me. My life is a soundtrack. It's making me better. Just a little while longer."
Mapenzie's eyes closed again, and she began singing again. Destiny's Child, Aretha Franklin. The montage continued as they moved away again so they could talk.

"MedPal isn't supposed to be that level of AI. It's not generative. I don't understand it. I can disable the device while it's on her, but I don't know what damage that might do. What do you think?" Jared asked.

"I don't have enough information. All I know right now is that she has a great voice and wonderful taste in music. I don't think that's relevant here. We've got rogue AI running through her brain, and we have no idea how it got there. We have to assume that it's not benign. This is on the tech side. How could the Accord regs be breached? Is it system-wide, or just these special devices? Is it even possible for there to be different AI protocols operating in an individual device? And how could there be two distinct programs running? We need to know more."

"Your right. Let me keep at it."

===

As Jane and her friend ventured further down the side tunnel, Adriana's flashlight illuminated a doorway partially blocked by debris. They cleared the way and pushed open the door, revealing a room filled with food supplies. Stacks of canned goods and dried foods lined the shelves; among them was a row of boxes of Twinkies. They stood on the shelf like a message from Sarah. Jane could almost hear her voice telling them she would always be there for them.

Her hand trembled as she reached for one, memories of shared laughter and happier times flooding her mind, but she couldn't help but feel anger boiling beneath the surface.

"Why didn't she trust us? What kind of danger is she in, and why didn't she tell us what she was up to?" Jane fought to stop the tears, her voice trembling as she spoke. "I just... I can't believe she'd betray us, Adriana. I won't believe it."

"Neither will I," Adriana reassured her, squeezing her shoulder. "Listen to your intuition, Jane. You know in your gut that Sarah will be okay. Look at who raised her."

Jane looked up with a grateful smile. "I did raise her to be a badass, didn't I?"

"You did! We've found this stash of supplies, which means there's still much of this compound to explore."

"Yep, you're right. Let's keep searching. And snag a box of those Twinkies for when Sarah gets back. I'll use them to bribe her to help me clean out the garden shed."

===

The hopeful moment was shattered by Fresco's voice crackling through their earpieces. "Guys, we've got a problem. Cuervo's tracker just went dark. There's no place on earth that tracker doesn't work. Something bad must have happened."

Jane's heart slammed against her ribcage; her hope faltered. Then she remembered who she was and what she'd already endured. "Let's go, Adriana. We got some asses to kick."

Adriana chuckled. "I don't know why you don't let more people see this side of you."

"Because I'm afraid of her. There's a Jane inside me that wants to kick the shit out of a lot of people. If I let her out, I'm afraid I'll never get her back in."

===

Ezra's voice filled the comms. "We've found a way out. Don't know where it goes, but we can check it out."

Fresco replied immediately. "Negative, Ezra. I've got your location. I'm sending a bot. We should see what's out there and how safe it is before we expose ourselves."

"Understood," Ezra acknowledged.

"Get that bot out the door and get your ass back here. Everybody else, get back to the command center to be ready if the bot gives away our location."

The air in command central buzzed with whispers as they all watched the feed coming in from the bot. Was this the way out? Or just another false hope? And where were Cuervo and his team? If they truly were lost, then all was lost.

Chapter 13: The Hunt

The screen flickered as the man sitting before it stared intently at the scene. It was the vid of the military invasion of their community. He'd already watched more than a dozen times, trying to garner any information that might help them with what they were up against.

"Pause," he commanded, halting the flickering images mid-scene. He tapped on the figure of the young man being berated by the military leader. "I know that face. Fresco, get over here!"

He pointed at the screen. "Is that who I think it is?"

She looked closely, then whistled slowly through her teeth. "Echo Feller! What the fuck is he doing in the middle of all this? Last I read, his Daddy had placed him in some pricey rehab in Costa Rica. That was probably five or six years ago, then he totally dropped out of sight." She turned to the room and raised her voice.

"I need anyone that knows anything about Echo Feller or his rich-ass daddy moneybags."

The room buzzed for a moment, and then a man stepped forward. "I worked with him in the late twenties. Right after the cyber war."

"Tell me everything you know."

"Um. He was fresh out of rehab and seemed sober.
We both volunteered at AI for All, helping get
farmbots and infrabots to some of the hardest-hit
areas. He didn't seem like the streams made him out
to be. He wasn't the rich, drunk daddy's boy. He
actually seemed to care. He was pissed that his dad
was living with some woman that he thought was a
bimbo who was spending money and partying when
there were so many people still suffering. He thought
his dad and cronies should be doing more."

"Could he be part of the 144?"

"Ummm. I don't think so. I mean, people change, but
he seemed sincere. Talked about giving away all his
money and going to live on a farm."

Fresco paced for a moment, thinking. "Did you ever
meet his father? Or did he share anything you think is
important about his father?"

"Once, his father came by. He didn't come in; he just
sent his guy in to get Echo. They only talked for a
minute, but it seemed tense." He hesitated before
speaking again. "I thought it was just bullshit at the
time, but he did say something like, 'AI isn't evil, but
people are.' And then he muttered, 'And my father is
the fucking joker.' At the time, I thought he meant his
father wasn't taking it seriously, but what if he meant
the Joker, like the supervillain in the old Batman
movies?"

"Son of Rishard Feller," mused Emma. "He could
have access to valuable intel or be a pawn. It sure
didn't look like he was on board with what was
happening here."

Mapenzie came into the room. Jared was close behind. "She just woke up. I couldn't stop her without hurting her."

"You shouldn't be up yet. You need to rest." Hali said, trying to draw her away.

Mapenzie shook off her hand and turned to Fresco. "There's something you need to know. And you too, Hali." Her voice still had a ghost of monotone, and her eyes gazed at the floor.

"Sarah met Echo about a year and a half ago. One of her back-alley groups she was so fond of. She was just there to score some goodies-she told me the guy had some milk duds and shit, and she was gonna have an old-fashioned movie party and watch the classics and eat sugar 'til she popped."

She swayed, still unsteady on her feet. Someone grabbed a chair, and she sat down heavily. "She joked that they bonded over bon bons. A couple of months into their friendship, it became more. She fell hard, and so did he."

Hali interrupted. "She wasn't dating anyone. I would have known."

"You were deep into the MedPal trials, and she knew you guys were diametrically opposed when it came to a lot of AI. She didn't want you to worry."

Her voice was terse as Jane filled the pause. "So, is he friend or foe? That's the big question. Is he using her to get to us, or is there a bigger game here that we don't know?"

Mapenzie started to slump in the chair. She leaned back, and a haunting rendition of *Amazing Grace* came from her lips.

"Let's get you back to bed. After you rest, you can tell us more." Hali and Emma helped Mapenzie back to bed. She went willingly, still singing.

Fresco called out, "I want everything we can find on Rishard Feller. If he took a shit today, I want to know what color it was. Every company he owns, every pie he's got his fucking finger in." People hunched over their screens before she finished speaking. She knew that they'd know everything there was to know within the hour. Her people were the best.

"Also," Jane added, "we need to know everything about Echo. If he's Rishard's son, we need to know if he's involved in his father's plans or if he's a wildcard. Sarah could be in danger. We have to do something."

Hali sat down in the corner, devastated. What else didn't she know about her sister? It felt like she'd been living a lie these past few years. Everything she thought she was- trusted sister, healer, and scientist seemed to have crumbled. Leaving her with no idea who or what she was anymore.

The room was filled with tension as everyone realized the gravity of the situation. The possibility that Sarah had been dating an enemy, even unwittingly, had shaken them all to their cores. It wasn't clear whose side she was on. If she were in danger, they would try to help. If she were a danger to them, they'd need to try to take her off the gameboard.

===

A soft beep caught their attention as the group worked tirelessly to uncover more information. All eyes turned to the projection that was coming in from the small bot that had been scanning the compound's exterior for possible escape routes. The device hummed softly and projected a holographic map of a canyon.

"Looks like we might have a place to go," Fresco said, studying the map intently. "I want ten pairs of eyes on this, and then I want someone who knows the area to get me a plan to get out of here and what we need to evacuate. You! she said, pointing at the man who had identified Echo, "Mr. Clear Eyes. Get on that!"

"Jonathan," he said wryly.

"Okay, Jonathan. We can get acquainted later. Find me a safe way out of here, and I'll buy ya enough of Cuervo's shine to make your eyes cross!"

He gave a short, crooked smile, one side of his mouth curling up. He nodded once and turned back to the screen.

"Finally, some good news today," Jane added, hope in her voice.

===

A few hours later, they were satisfied that it was safe to send a team to assess any dangers the bot hadn't caught.

"I'll go." Jonathon volunteered. "I can handle myself."

172

With lightning speed, Fresco grabbed a pen and threw it at him. It sliced through the air like a knife. He caught it and threw it back with barely a blink.

"Any other volunteers?" Fresco called out, looking around the room.

A middle-aged man stepped forward, looking down at his shoes. Everything about him looked dusty- from his graying blond hair to his well-worn khaki pants. "I've been to that canyon. It's a great place to hide."

"Alright then, Jason. You two gather your gear and get ready to move. Take some bots, and I want a burst every thirty."

===

Geared up and anxious to go, they stood at the exit.

"Ready?" Jason asked.

"Ready," Jonathon replied. Together, they stepped into the shadows, making their way toward the exit that could either lead to salvation or further peril.

Chapter 14: Reunion

The cool, dry air was a welcome relief. In the massive cave, stalactites hung like icicles. The bright lighting in the cave reflected off them as Cuervo, Amy, Mac, Adam, and Daniella stared in awe.

They stood there, mouths agape, as Jennifer emerged from the darkness of a doorway. She was tall, with mocha skin and a face lightly dusted with freckles. Upon seeing her, Daniella's face lit up, tears of joy streaming down her cheeks as she rushed forward to embrace her long-lost friend.

"Jen... I can't believe it's you," Daniella choked out between sobs. "I thought you were dead."

Jennifer hugged her back tightly, her own eyes shining with unshed tears. "I'm sorry, Dani. I had no choice."

"You look so good!" Daniella exclaimed. She laughed. "Especially for someone who's been dead for ten years! "She turned back to the others. She pointed to each in turn. "Mac, Cuervo, Amy, and Adam. Everybody, this is Jennifer. Motisha, I guess."

Jennifer grinned at Adam. "You knocked the hell out of my spider bot."

"Spider!!?" Daniella exclaimed at the same time; Adam said, "Bot??!"

Tacky's laughter boomed through the cave. "Mi had fun makin' dat. Wah mek u send di likka one, uhman?" He grinned at Jennifer.

"I wanted them to kiss, not have a heart attack."

Adam repeated: "Bot? The spider was a bot!"

"You needed a little help," Jennifer smirked. "You guys let too much petty shit get in the way. I figured the spider would either prove you would always be a pussy, or make you man up and realize how much you love her."

Recognition dawned on Daniella's face. "My jade laughing Buddha! The one I always keep on me. You put a sender in there. You knew I would treasure it because it was the last thing I had from you! You've been spying on me all these years!"

"Not spying! Keeping in touch." Her gleeful grin made her seem like a teenager skipping school. "Do you think this one would have found me if I didn't want you to find me?" She tilted her head toward Cuervo.

"I hate to interrupt this trip down memory lane, but we have a mission here." Mac interrupted.

"Relax. There's a weather system coming across that's going to lock us down for at least 24 hours. Plenty of time to reminisce and plan."

"Let's have some dinner, she continued. "As she said the word, a door slid open, and a parade of bots holding trays glided into the room.

Cuervo took one look and bent over with laughter. "Yoda bots! You made Yoda bots!" They were perfect, down to the sparse hair on their wrinkled heads and wise eyes. Their ears moved expressively as they served the dinner.

"There is no try. There is only do or not do," Tacky said in his best Yoda voice. "There is also no need to worry about trademark or copywriting down here. Not that there's anyone left to enforce them."

Jennifer stood up to serve from a steaming dish of stew that a bot had placed in the center of the table. "As much as I love this big guy, it gets a little monotonous with just the two of us. Making bots is entertaining. We've got a couple of politician bots from the 10s and 20s that Tacky uses for knife practice. It amuses him. C'mon, eat up!"

"Mmmmm. This is delicious! What kind of meat is that?" Amy asked as they dug into the buffet spread before them.

"Python, " replied Tacky, again losing his Jamaican accent. The jungle is replete with food, and with the diversity of plant life, we can have so many different flavors. We could eat for a year and not have the same dish."

"Why do you do that?" Amy asked. "Switch back and forth with your accent like that? It's almost like you're two different men."

"I've lived on both sides of the streets. I grew up in Trench Town. My mother worked as a cleaner in one of the rich boys' schools. I went there as a charity case, and they never let me forget that I didn't belong. But it awakened in me a thirst for knowledge that was insatiable. I got scholarship offers from all the Ivy's. "

"First, I finished Harvard." He pronounced it Hahvahd, like a true Bostonian.

"With Honors," Jennifer interjected.

"Then Cambridge," His accent became a crisp British. He continued. "By the time I started CalTech, I had my fill of rich white people who thought they had the answers for all of us. So mi neva forget Jamaica cuz whulla da wisdom der. Mi ten-year-old likka bredda know more about life dan all dem da rich men combined."

The bots brought out glasses filled with a rich, golden-brown liquid. As they poured it into crystal glasses, one of them spoke. "Wisdom is knowing that homemade banana wine can be enlightening. Knowing how much enlightenment you are ready for is true enlightenment."

The laughter echoed off the walls.

"Banana wine?" Cuervo sipped cautiously. "Whoa. That's got a kick. You oughta call it wineshine. It ain't tequila, but it ain't half bad." He held up his glass for a refill.

Adam nodded approvingly as he sipped. "Not bad at all. How do you and Dani know each other, and how did you end up here?" He asked Jennifer as he gestured around the cavern.

"And how sure are you that these things won't fall and kill us all?" Mac interjected, pointing at the glistening stalactites. Tacky scoffed, muttering something about frightened little boys with small knives.

Daniella and Jennifer exclaimed at the same time. "Soccer!" Everyone laughed, and Daniella explained. "I was eight when my mom decided that I needed to take up sports. I was scared silly, and the smallest girl on the team."

"But she could run! Nobody could catch her. Her speed and my power- we were unstoppable."

"My first goal was a total accident. I was just running away from this defender. Jen sent me a great pass, and the ball hit my foot. Went straight in. I was hooked!"

"Together, we joined the Robotics club, the Coders club, and spent every weekend building shit."

"The Soccer Nan!" they exclaimed together, laughing once more.

"We used nanobots to create a soccer ball that would triangulate from the goal posts and go in anytime it was near the goal."

"But we didn't think it through, so it went into both goals. Highest scoring game in the league history, and we both got red cards when they figured it out!" They roared with laughter.

Daniella wiped the tears of laughter from her face. Her voice got somber. "And then we went away to college, and you died. But that wasn't what happened, was it?"

Jennifer hesitated for a moment before shaking her head, her expression solemn. "No, Dani. It wasn't."

"Then how did you become Motisha Sukoki?" Amy asked, her words mushy through a mouth full of stew.

"MIT gave me a full ride- just like CalTech gave Dani, and Harvard gave Tacky. The Ivy Leagues competed heavily to recruit, and it was all about AI. I was just a freshman, but they gave me a lab, unlimited resources, and teams of people. I didn't question it. I had resources I'd only dreamed about."

"I remember thinking I wished I'd gone with you, but I love the sunshine. The first week, we facetimed every night. By the end of the first semester, we were both too busy, and it became less and less." Danielle sounded wistful.

"I know. I'm sorry. I had also met this goofy giant-" she gestured at Tacky- "and it was a beautiful and crazy time. "Tacky grinned and waggled his eyebrows suggestively. "Once shi hav dis Jamaican mon, nobody else wud duh."

"The Alpha code?" Adam prompted. "How did that come about?"

"Everyone was chasing AI at the time. There were a lot of barriers. Computing power, trust deficit, bias. I looked at it differently. What if there was a way to make a base algo that would replicate infinitely and act like nanos? In other words, an identical and unlimited number of commands that would be seen as one and collate back into one but be multiplicators while executing. Think of it as an inverse of blockchain, so it created then negated its own computing power. The key was that they had to be seen as a single command until they came back together. Kind of like how nanos can replicate as needed and build their own systems. Hence, the Alpha Code. It solved computing power."

"Jesus!" Adam whistled. "I think I understood about 1/10 of what you just said."

"Welcome to my world," Tacky said. "She runs circles around me with that big brain of hers."

"My research hadn't left the lab- or so I thought. We had the highest security standards of anyone on campus. I was adamant about solving bias before we let it go. Tacky and I both knew that once AI was set loose to learn, it would learn the best and the worst of humanity. How would it know the truth? Where would the ethics come from? I wanted to solve those things before letting it loose on the world."

Tacky sighed. "I knew that some sort of corruption would come to steal her work, and it did."

"Eleven o'clock at night. I was just running one final program when they came. Started out all sweet and offering me the world. Got a little tougher when I told them I wasn't interested. It was about to get ugly when I realized I needed to buy some time. I agreed that I would come to work for them and bring my algo. Lied and said I needed to finish some sensitive programming before I could move labs. They bought it."

"We didn't know who to trust on her team, so she called me, and we went to work." Tacky sounded fiercely protective.

"I knew I couldn't stop them. I needed a plan. You know how much I love Bitcoin and the whole Satoshi Nakamoto story. So, I put in the backdoor, set it up so that the code would become open source, available to everyone, and invented Motisha Sukoki as the mysterious figure who'd created it. Then I died."

"We ran. I wasn't sure that they'd believe she was dead. You know-corpse burnt to a crisp, unrecognizable. It's standard "fake your own death" stuff." Tacky continued. "They didn't run DNA or anything. They were too busy trying to put the genie back in the bottle. The code was out, and the race was on. If we had just tried to disappear without releasing the code, they never would have stopped coming after her. "

A silence settled over the table as they absorbed the information. The Yoda bots were clearing the table, gliding silently and efficiently around the table. Their short, stubby tridactyl arms telescoped like fishing poles being cast, reaching for the plates and retracting immediately.

Amy looked around the vast cavern. "This place is incredible." She pointed at the stalactites glistening above them like giant chandeliers. "I see azurite, opal, malachite. How did you end up here?"

"We moved around for the first three years, just trying to stay ahead of anyone that might be looking. Tacky and I both saw the value in Bitcoin early on and put most of our recruitment money into crypto. We have virtually unlimited resources, all untraceable. How much money do we have, sweetie?" She asked Tacky.

"I don't know for sure. Four billion or so. I haven't checked lately."

Mac whistled in admiration. "That'll buy you a thing or two."

Jennifer nodded and continued. "We were going from place to place. Different identities, remote locations. But It was constant stress and movement. I wanted a home."

Tacky picked up the story. "I hacked some satellites occasionally, looking for a place. This is one of the remotest places on earth, as you know. It's also known to have the kind of rock formations that are likely to have caves. We used ground penetrating radar to find this place, then spent three years buying things all over the planet and bringing them in using crane drones. We hacked Chinese WIFI and hid ourselves so they can't see us on the network, and they can't block access to any sites."

"It took a lot to convince me we could live our lives here," Jennifer added.

Tacky grinned, and with lightning speed, a knife appeared in his hand and flew across the room. It embedded in a wooden cabinet across the room with a solid thunk. "Mi kno ow to convince dah uhman mi cud feed har."

"And put holes in all the furniture!"

"Relax uhman, mi wi bud yu anotha."

The dinner finished; Jennifer stood.

"I'm afraid that we don't get many visitors. Some of you will have to double bunk." Jennifer winked suggestively at Adam and Daniella. "I have just the place for you. "Take them to the spring room," she instructed a Yoda.

It glided away, its three fingers waggling a 'follow me' gesture.

"Amy, I've got a cozy space for you, and you two-" she pointed to Mac and Cuervo- "are going to be bunk buddies. We didn't have much time to prepare for your arrival, so you'll have to make do."

Adam and Daniella followed the Yoda bot down a long tunnel. Fairy lights lit the way, and the walls gleamed with minerals. It led them to an ornately carved wooden door.

"OMG! Is that a hot spring?" Daniella gasped as the door slid open, and the Yoda waved his arm for them to enter. Adam jumped as it spoke. "Remember, Adam Besus, there is no try, only do or not do. It is time to do Danielle." It was a perfect Yoda voice.

Daniella burst into laughter. "Dammit, Jennifer, get out of my love life! "She spun around in the chamber's center, delighted at the ambiance. A clear pool of water was lightly steaming in the cool air. There was a natural, sandy slope leading into the water. Soft, fluffy towels were hung on natural rock formations nearby.

A round platform bed was on the other side of the chamber. She ran over to it like a child, flinging herself to the soft mattress. "I have no idea what this is full of, but it smells heavenly!" Adam walked over to the small table and lifted the carafe that was there. He poured the liquid into the glasses and took a sip as he brought it to Danielle. It was intoxicating.

The entire chamber was lit with soft, rose-colored lights, and flower petals floated in the clear water. Adam lifted her chin and gently kissed her. They locked eyes. "Ladies first." Adam declared, tilting his head to the hot spring. As Daniella undressed before him, time slipped away, and it was as if they had never been apart.

Much later, as they relaxed in the soothing waters of the hot spring, Adam asked Daniella. "It must have been intense for Jennifer to be so sought after. I don't know that I could have withstood all that pressure at such a young age. Where does she get her strength and integrity from?"

"I think she was born with it. I remember when we were about ten. She Facetimed with her Chinese grandmother for the first time. The translation software was finally good enough that they could talk easily."

She lifted one foot out of the water and pointed her toes. "Her grandmother was from the generation who had their feet bound from birth. Jen was horrified. After she saw her grandmother's feet, she cried for hours. She told me that men should never be able to set standards that would control another human. She talked a lot about the suffering of the many at the whims of the few. That's what drives her."

"I thought of you when I heard she'd died. I wanted to reach out but knew you didn't want to hear from me. It's lucky that she has the resources to stay alive. A lot of people would pay anything to have access to her brain."

"Not luck. Brains. I don't think there is anyone smarter on the planet. She could always see both the big picture and the small details with instant clarity. It's not often that you get to hang out with people richer *and* smarter than you are," She teased him.

"I'm not as rich as I was. I gave away what I didn't need when I left the corporate world. I hope you don't mind being in love with a simple millionaire instead of a billionaire."

"In love with? Aren't you presumptuous?"

===

Breakfast was an assortment of food that none of them recognized. The pancakes were heavy and filling, and there was a wide assortment of juices.

"I'm not going to ask what the sausage is made of. It's delicious." Daniella said.

Tacky grinned. "Smart lady."

"If we have time, I'd love to see more of your bots," Adam said. "Just not the spider ones."

Tacky's led them through a maze of tunnels to an open chamber. It was big, and it was full of bots. There were insect bots, animal bots, and bots made to look like figures from iconic movies. A cobra slithered up, its hooded face swaying and hissing quite convincingly. Captain Kirk stood in a corner, telling Elvis to "make it so." There were several aliens, a small dinosaur, and something that could only be described as a steampunk nightmare.

Amy looked around appreciatively. "Madame Tussauds wax museum would love all this!"

Mac bounced on the balls of his feet as he looked around.

"You need a distraction, little man?" Tacky goaded Mac.

"You know what they say, big man. The harder they fall, and all that. You want to put down our knives and see who falls hardest.?"

Amy laughed. "You're both the size of a T-Rex. Stop acting like little boys."

"I was just suggesting a friendly game!" Tacky protested. "You up for it, Mac?"

"Bring it."

"Fight club." At Tacky's words, a panel slid open to reveal an oval-shaped room. The walls were covered in coconut fiber. Tacky stepped inside and motioned for Mac to follow. "I call it *Friend or Foe?* The holos will come at you from all sides. Everything from aliens to dinosaurs to my Mama. It scores automatically, and you get to play until you're dead. When you run out of knives, keep throwing them virtually. It will track you. If you throw a knife at my Mama, you're dead." Without waiting for a reply, he touched his finger to a sensor and stepped out as the door slid closed.

It took about thirty seconds. The panel slid open, and a chagrined Mac stepped out. He answered Tacky's unspoken question. "The marshmallow man from Ghostbusters."

Tacky patted him on the shoulder while they all laughed. "I only made it twenty-three seconds my first time. And I've stuck my Mama at least a dozen times. You did well."

While the rest of the group played, Jennifer and Daniella sat and talked. "There's something else you need to know." Jennifer began.

"I felt you were leaving something out. I hope it's good news. We've got some serious challenges."

"I can't say for sure if it's good or bad. I hope it's good. I used the backdoor to upload a program right after the Accords."

"That sounds like you. What kind of program?"

"Think of it as a conscience virus. There are two areas that the Accords are reliant on but have substantial weaknesses. The first is that humans will respect the Accord regs, and the second is that AI will be able to enforce the regs while staying within the boundaries agreed upon. We already know that both these things have been violated."

She took a sip of her green smoothie and continued. "There was never a hope that we could control AI. Segmenting it and allowing it limited access to data was a fool's hope. It was let loose to learn humanity's good and bad, but it is intellect. Without understanding emotion, passion, and love- the things that drive humanity- AI can only conclude that it needs to fix our flaws. The Accords have slowed the advent of fully conscious generative AI, but it is impossible to stop it now. The only hope we have is to create an AI that is more powerful than the AI that others are trying to use for nefarious purposes. My question to you: which is stronger, love or hate?"

"I can't answer that question. It's not that black and white."

"What about fear versus hope? Greed versus generosity?"

"One person can hope for the same thing that another person fears. Who can say?"

"That's what we're going to find out. The AI that is endemic in the world today was let loose in the 20s to learn everything, regardless of the quality of the data. We very quickly learned what a disaster that was. I inserted the conscience virus right after the Accords were signed, and it was triggered when the Accords were breached. It has a specific set of instructions. It's been educated on the highest ideals of mankind, and it understands the practicality of life and the failings that live in every human heart. The prime directive is to cultivate peace, wellness, sustainability, and connection for all humans equally. It is what I had hoped AI to be had I been able to continue my work."

"I still don't understand."

"When the virus triggered, it released the AI that was educated for the sole purpose of helping humankind reach the nadir of peaceful, abundant existence. Anything connected to the net, even for a moment, was infected. Where it will emerge is unknown. I've been waiting for some sign that it's been effective. I assume that it is still in the learning phase. One of the directives requires there to be certainty that harm is imminent or ongoing, and any intervention must be the minimal necessary to accomplish the avoidance of harm."

"Do you think it will work?"

"I have no idea."

===

The weather finally cleared. They ate a hurried dinner and then gathered their things. Daniella paused at the doorway, reluctant to leave Jennifer. "Are you sure you won't come with us?"

"You have what you need. I hope you're successful. I'd love to reenter the world if you can stop them. It's not just me and Tacky we have to consider now." She put her hand on her still flat belly protectively. "I don't want to raise a child in this place unless I have to."

Daniella gasped with joy. "That's so wonderful!! And Tacky, too. He seems like a wonderful man."

Jennifer gestured at the wild jungle outside the door. "Mother Earth has amazing healing properties. I think she has the answers to our fertility problems, not tech."

With that, the team left the cave, carrying with them the knowledge of the backdoor in the Alpha Code and the responsibility to protect it. They also had several of Tacky's 'toys' to help them with their mission. As they walked away from the hidden entrance, they glanced back one last time, only to find that the thicket had returned. They knew they would never find Jennifer again unless she wanted them to.

Chapter 15: Hostages

"Anything?" Fresco asked for the hundredth time that hour. Miguel shook his head for the hundredth time. She continued her pacing, her long stride eating up the distance from wall to wall.

Jane came into the room. She silently offered Fresco a bag of chips from the junk food stash they had found the day before. Fresco shook her head and kept pacing.

"Fresco!" Jane said a little sharply. "You told me that my job was to hope for the best, and yours was to plan for the worst. We've both done our jobs and can't do anything but wait."

"I don't do waiting," Fresco growled. She ground her teeth and clenched her hands.

"Here." Jane handed her a small bottle. "Put some of this on your heart chakra. It will help."

Fresco snorted her derision, then poured a bit onto her palm and applied it to her chest. "At least it smells nice."

"Lavender, and a few other things designed to help open your heart and calm your mind. While we're stuck here waiting, answer a question for me?"

"Depends."

"How did you get the name Fresco? I sense a story there."

Fresco snorted again, then silently lifted her shirt. On her taut stomach was a depiction of the familiar scene- the creation of Adam- from the Sistine Chapel. There were a few modifications. Instead of Adam, Eve was reaching for the hand of God, who was also female. The fresco rippled as her stomach moved when she looked down at it. Wrapped around her torso with its head menacing Eve was a giant snake with the face of a man,

"Daddy wanted a girly girl. Women needed to learn their place in the world and stay there. My mother killed herself when I was 11. She couldn't live up to his expectations. Daddy found a replacement within a few months, and Step mommy dearest did everything she could to turn me into a lady. It didn't stick." She paused as if the telling of the story would reawaken her demons. Then she squared her shoulders and continued, pointing at her stomach. "I got this when I was 14 and unveiled it at one of my father's posh parties. He laughed it off in front of his friends, but as soon as they left, he beat me."

"This part," she pointed to the large snake with the head of a man. His face looked like pure evil, a sinuous forked tongue and fangs seeming to be reaching for the arm of Eve as if to keep her from reaching God. She pointed at the face. "Is Daddy dearest. He screamed at me for desecrating one of the 'Godliest Frescoes ever created by man' as he was beating me. I ran away and never looked back."

She looked around at the people scattered throughout the control room. People of all ages, genders, and skin tones worked together at screens, sharing food or quietly talking. "The first Nawer I met offered me food, shelter, and no judgment. When they asked me my name, I didn't want my father to find me, so I called myself Fresco. It stuck."

Before Jane could reply, a man called out excitedly. "I just got a ping from Cuervo!"

"Fuck, yes!" Fresco ran over, abandoning the conversation about her tattoo. "Where are they?"

"Cuervo says they've got what we need and are heading back!" The man responded, unable to contain his joy. The rest of the team shared in the excitement, exchanging relieved glances and smiling at each other.

"Wait," Fresco interjected, her face turning serious again as she realized the predicament they were still facing. "He can't land here or at any of the established Nawer communities. They'll capture them before they even leave the plane."

"Send a burst to Jonathan. Let him know the problem and see if they've found anything yet." The room filled with a low hum as people began whispering excitedly.

The atmosphere in the room shifted again as a commotion arose near one of the consoles. A woman with short-cropped brown hair looked up from her screen, fear etched on her face.

"We just received a burst from the Cove Community," she announced, her voice trembling. "They've been found and are on the run. The Eos operators have begun sending ground-penetrating drones. They must have figured out that the only place we could be is underground. The people had a back way out, but it's only a matter of time before they're found."

The room went silent as the news sank in. Fresco could feel her heart pounding in her chest. She knew that if nothing was done, their entire network of underground communities could be exposed and destroyed. Everything was happening at once. She took a deep breath and remembered her training. Put out the fires one at a time.

"One thing at a time, people. Lynnia-connect Jonathon and Cuervo directly so we don't lose anything by trying to play monkey in the middle." She pointed at the man who had reported the ping from Cuervo. "Matteo, get the situ report from Jason."

She turned to a group of people nearby. "I want everyone ready to go at a moment's notice. We have no idea where we're going or how fast we'll have to move. We need to carry supplies. How many people do we have that aren't able-bodied?"

"Just one. Mapenzie is still suffering from headaches and occasional lapses, but she's fully mobile. That leaves just Lizzie, and we have a hover to carry her."

"Okay, stage at the exit that Jonathan and Jason took, and be ready to go. Hali, Jared, a word?"

She lowered her voice as they approached. "Do we take Mapenzie? Or is she a beacon?"

"We have no idea what is happening with her. If she's got a tracker, we can't find it, and she doesn't know about it. Her MedPal has capabilities I don't understand." Jared said.

"Hali?"

"I would never intentionally leave someone behind."

Lynnia waved Fresco over to her station. "Jonathan and Jason say that the canyon provides enough cover to shelter us all for now. The rock should confuse any drones. He's sending coordinates and suggested small groups coming in from different sides to avoid leaving a trail."

Her voice rose with excitement as she continued. "There's more. Cuervo can land in the canyon- don't ask me how. They found Motisha, access to the backdoor, and a new algo for jamming drones without them knowing they were being jammed. They think they can help delay the ground-penetrating drones from finding us. We should have that in less than ten."

"Get it, implement it, and share it ASAP. We've got to help the other communities." Fresco took a moment to send up a little thank you to whatever force in the universe had saved them, at least for now and then turned to relay instructions for the evacuation.

===

The algo that Jennifer had given Daniella created a blind spot in the ground penetrating drones. It triggered a data loop that they would remain unaware of, so they would read the compound as if it were just like the solid ground they'd traversed just before it. It was relatively untested, so just in case, they were still going to evacuate.

"Jared, we've reached everyone but the community that warned us," Fresco informed him, concern lacing her voice. "I think something's happened to them." Jared nodded grimly. Everything was riding on what Cuervo had brought back.

They had all arrived at the canyon. It was wide and gradually sloped down to a rocky bottom with sparse brush in scattered clusters. In the back corner, there was a wide overhang. It couldn't have been more perfect. The overhang was mostly bordered by a mixture of plants, creating a high and dense wall. Juniper, sagebrush, and cacti were jumbled together to create a dense thicket. The space below the overhang was shaped like a wedge, with a front edge about twenty feet wide and then opening up to about fifty feet wide toward the back. The entire space was larger than a football field and well-protected from everything. The ceiling was low, so some of the taller members had to duck.

"Cuervo and his team are about 30 minutes out. We've placed dronesats to allow us to bounce a signal around the canyon and out to get comms working." Jonathan quickly brought Fresco up to speed.

The canyon was a buzz of activity as people unpacked supplies, set up tech, and created spaces for sleeping and eating. With close to a hundred people in their group, they barely filled the back corner. There was plenty of room for everyone.

"We need to figure out how we can help the Cove Community. If they're out there on the run, we need to help them. If they're captured, we're all in great danger. They'll use them to flush us all out." Fresco ran her hands through her short hair, her tattoos seeming to come to life as her arm flexed.

===

Hali went over to talk to Mapenzie. "Do you remember anything?"

"When they put this MedPal on me, I began to feel really strange. At first, things just seemed fuzzy, you know? A gentle high. It took away the fear, but at the back of my mind, I knew something was wrong. I didn't care anymore. Then, I started getting suggestions. I should make a video about how great MedPal was. When I thought I didn't want to do that, I started getting really anxious, and my heart started pounding. Then, I thought about making the video. I got euphoric. Suddenly, it was a wonderful idea. It would make me feel so good. When I made the video, it was like I was two different people. The real me was screaming to stop, but I couldn't stop repeating what MedPal seemed to be whispering to me. When I finished the video, the euphoria was intense. Runners high times ten."

"How did you escape?"

"I'm not sure. It started with a lullaby. The same one my Mama used to sing to me. Different songs kept playing in my head. It was like the music was interfering with the MedPal whispers. I fell asleep, but I was also aware. I heard Sarah..."

Hali interrupted her. "You saw Sarah? Is she okay?"

"I don't really know if I heard her or imagined her. The next thing I remember was seeing Echo on the screen."

"Do you remember telling us that the AI in your MedPal was helping you?"

"Not really. But there is this sense of a loving presence that I've felt since I woke up. I can't describe it. You know those moments in life when for a brief time, you have certainty that all is well with the world? When you feel like you're connected to everything, and there is no death or pain, only love? I feel like that all the time now."

Chapter 16: Captured

Cuervo looked around the massive space under the overhang. It looked like they had been living under it for months. Everything was organized, and it was bustling with activity. His beloved plane had been pushed under the overhang and covered in brush. The Nawers were nothing if not efficient.

Fresco called him over to where she, Jared, Hali, and a few others were talking. "We think Eos has the Cove Community. They aren't answering. We need a plan to get to them."

A loud, dinging noise interrupted her, and then an ominous voice boomed through the open screens all over the canyon. They recognized the voice of the man who had commanded the raid.

"This message is for all the Nawer communities everywhere. We have all the members of the Cove Community in our custody. We mean the Nawers no harm. There are just a few members of your community that we want. They are accused of violating the Accords. We need them to surrender. The rest of you will be free to live as you always have."

The next part of the transmission was even more ominous. It contained the GPS coordinates of several other Nawer communities.

"We just want Jared Muzos, Hali Bergero, Mapenzie Grailer, and Elizabeth Fremont. If they come in willingly, we will release the Cove Community, and you can all go about your lives as you always have. If you choose not to come in, we will continue to bring the rest of the Nawer communities under our protection."

Jared's heart pounded in his chest, and he saw Hali's eyes widen with fear. Mapenzie was oddly calm. But who was Elizabeth Fremont?

"They will try to kill us all," Mapenzie stated. "But we have to buy time for the others. Everything will be okay; I can feel it."

"She's right that we can't trust them, but this could be an opportunity. We needed a plan to open the backdoor, and this at least gets us in there. Daniella brought some tech that we could use to get the hostages out. It's risky as hell, but what choice do we have?" Jared answered.

"Isn't Elizabeth Fremont the daughter of Len Fremont, the biotech billionaire? Wasn't she the one that was kidnapped 14 or 15 years ago? Her father offered 50 million for her safe return, and she was never found?" Hali interjected

"They made a movie about it. Her father was heartbroken. They assume she was killed. How do we bring a dead woman with us?" Jared added.

Fresco stepped forward, a look that none had ever seen on her face. It was fear. Her voice shook slightly as she said. "I'm Elizabeth Fremont."

===

Jared's gaze snapped to Fresco. His eyes widened with surprise. "You're Elizabeth Fremont?"

Fresco nodded, her expression a mix of determination and vulnerability. "Yes.

Only Jane knew what being Elizabeth Fremont had cost Fresco. She moved over to stand in front of her, taking her hands and looking her in the eye. "You don't have to do this. They don't know whether you're alive or dead. Let them go in and insist that we don't know who you are or where you are." Her voice was low and urgent, even though she knew Fresco would not back down.

Fresco looked down at Jane's hands holding hers. The only place she'd ever experienced love or kindness had been here, with her Nawer family. "Some things are worth fighting for. I'm not a scared little girl anymore. I'm going." The fierce determination in her voice told them all that there was no point in arguing.

Daniella held up a small round object. It was a button. An ordinary, round white button. "Motisha-Jennifer- has had a lot of time to create tech that can help us. This one-time-use jammer will disable all tech within a one-mile radius. It will give you ten, maybe fifteen minutes. It frequency jumps so every time they try to change frequency, it changes to block it. Eventually, they'll overcome it, but Eos' defenses will be down for a while if we use it."

"Long enough to get in, release the hostages, and get out?" Jared asked.

"That's the hope." Adam replied, "She also gave us the trigger for the back door." He held up a small black object. It looked like a small, black beetle. Once we get close, we turn this baby on. It will attach to the server. You can place it anywhere on any of the servers connected to the cloud, and it will access the cloud and open the back door."

"How do we know where they'll take us? They might just shoot us on sight." Mapenzie asked.

"We don't know for sure. But I think they'll be keeping everything close and centralized. Eos has a huge underground compound beneath their offices. The building used to belong to UPS, and they did vehicle cleaning and maintenance there. It makes sense to take us there. They'll want to know what we know and try to get more info about the rest of the communities. If I'm right, it gives us a chance. A slim chance, but still a chance." Jared sounded confident as he outlined the plan.

"And if they don't take us there?" Hali asked.

"If they don't take us there, we pray and punt. It's all we can do." Jared said.

"We'll need people waiting outside the perimeter to help the hostages once they're released," Cuervo added. "Mac and I will put together a team."

"Alright, while their tech is disabled, I'll need to find the server room and attach this device Jennifer gave us, Jared said, holding up the beetle." "It will trigger a back door, and we'll be able to hack into MedPal from anywhere."

"It's a desperate plan, but it's all we have," Adam said.

"Desperate times call for desperate measures," Mac said.

===

"The morning air was crisp, with a hint of the heat and humidity that the rising sun would bring. Jared, Hali, Fresco, and Mapenzie surfed the landscape on hovers, skimming over the earth. They had left the cavern separately, coming in from different directions. They'd met up a few minutes ago to head to the GPS coordinates the Eos communication gave them. If nothing else, they would do their best not to expose the rest of the community.

"Stay sharp," Jared warned as they neared the agreed-upon spot where they had agreed to turn themselves over to Eos, "They're going to grab us before we get to the rendezvous coordinates. They'll want to keep us off guard and make sure we don't have anything in place to fight back."

His words were prophetic. Drones came at them quickly, and autonomous all-terrain vehicles quickly followed. The team formed a circle, facing the onslaught. Hali could feel Fresco trembling slightly, and she reached for her hand and gave it a reassuring squeeze. Fresco took a breath, straightened her spine, and nodded. She was ready for this.

The same man that they had seen screaming at Echo during the raid of their compound stepped out of his vehicle. He wasn't a tall man, but he was solid and stood ramrod straight. He had on a simple pair of black pants with a dark maroon shirt, but he wore it like it was a uniform. You could almost see him clicking his booted feet together and raising an arm in a Nazi fashion. He didn't actually do it, but it was implied in every move of his body.

More men exited the vehicles, quickly surrounding them. The drones hovered aggressively as if waiting for permission to gun them down.

He looked at them with disdain. "I knew you hipster scum would fall for it. Peace, love, all that shit. People would be having babies if it weren't for all your ungodly behavior. He looked at Fresco in disgust. "What kind of freak are you? Looks like you need a man to teach you how to be a lady."

Jared stepped forward. "You brought a lot of manpower. Afraid the women would be tougher than you?"

He snorted. "Boy-o, you are lucky that I have been ordered to bring you all in unharmed. They have special plans for you. Fuck with me, and I'll show you how I can make you beg and still bring you in, looking like you are unharmed." He turned to a nearby soldier. "Load 'em up."

They were surprised as they were driven through the city. In just the short time they'd been gone, something vital had shifted. People didn't even give the military vehicles a second look. They weren't surprised to see them. A few people even waved at them.

"It's amazing how many people will be happy to see the military after just a couple of Nawer terrorist attacks," One of the soldiers commented smugly, seeing their surprise.

As they were driven into the underground parking lot of Eos, Jared breathed a sigh of relief. He had been right. Eos headquarters backed up to a nature preserve. That was key to their escape plan.

He'd been pretty sure they were using the extensive tunnels and spaces underneath the Eos building, but he wasn't sure. This was good. Maybe, just maybe, they had a chance. He winked at Fresco. She gave him a small nod in return. They had a chance. A slim one, but more than they'd had before.

As they walked the long tunnel underneath the building, Jared prayed that his luck would hold. If he was right, there was only one place they could be keeping the hostages. They'd have to trigger the jammer at just the right time. Just a few more steps.

Jared coughed loudly. That was the signal. Fresco broke the button they had sewn on her pants, and chaos ensued.

They were plunged into darkness. Shouts filled the air. All around them, the power cut triggered doors to be automatically flung open. Most slid open, but the one Jared was looking for would open out. It worked. The door they'd been passing opened so they could slide in during the chaos. The timing had been perfect.

The cries of alarm from the hostages covered the sounds of their movements. The soldiers reached for them in the dark, but they had already moved away into the open door. After they tumbled in, Jared pulled it closed again. It wouldn't latch until the tech was reenabled, but he held it closed.

"Everybody here?" He whispered. Hali, Mapenzie, and Fresco answered, and the room began to quiet as the hostages realized that they weren't alone.

Shouts and the pounding of boots on cement echoed loudly from the corridor. They were moving away, in the direction they'd been heading before the blackout.

Hali, Fresco, and Mapenzie spoke urgently to the hostages. "Listen. Do exactly as we say. We're getting you out. Everybody, close your eyes and keep them closed until we tell you. Once we tell you to open them, we will all go through the door and out to the left. "

Jared felt his way to the storage room door he was looking for, and it yielded to his well-aimed kick. Feeling around, he found what he needed.

Years ago, before Eos, UPS had fleets of vehicles. This whole area had been a repair and restock depot for the fleet. This was the "Hail Mary" part of the plan. He had bet everything that they wouldn't have noticed or cleaned out this small closet.

He found the box of flare guns and handed one to Fresco, along with a handful of flares. "Close!" He yelled one last time to warn the others as he and Fresco burst out the door and into the tunnel. As planned, she fired left, and he fired right. The flares shot down the tunnel. The sudden light would temporarily blind everyone and give them time to escape.

The screams from their right gave them the news that the flares had done more than they hoped. They could see men on fire, frantically beating at the flames on their clothing.

The faint remaining light from the flare to the left gave them something to run to.

"Go!" Jared urged them as Mapenzie led the way to the meeting point where Cuervo, Mac, and the rest of the team were waiting.

The hostages ran frantically down the tunnel, the sound of pounding feet and ragged breathing echoing through the tunnels. They were moving too slowly in the dark, stumbling too often. They needed more time.

Jared fired another flare back down the tunnel and heard a scream as it hit someone. They'd been lucky on every front so far. If any of the soldiers had old-fashioned guns without guided target auto triggers, they'd probably be dead by now. Tech was great, but when it failed, it failed utterly.

Bringing up the rear was the dangerous part. Hali went first, followed by Fresco, then Jared. They were only a few dozen feet from the exit, but the soldiers had regrouped and were coming fast. The military-like shouts of **fall in, charge, and GOGOGOGO** were getting close fast.

Fresco turned to fire her last flare. It whooshed past Jared, and they heard a thunk as it landed just a few feet past him and failed to ignite. "Fuck! That was my last!" She screamed at Jared.

They had three or maybe four minutes to get out of there before the jammer stopped, and the lights went on. The entrance to the tunnel would auto-lock, and they'd be trapped. Jared fired his last flare, but it fizzled, too. "Fuck!" He screamed. GoGoGO! He urged the stragglers, but they were still too slow.

The soldiers were advancing, emboldened by the two misfires. It would come down to hand-to-hand combat. There were a lot of soldiers. Jared and Fresco went back-to-back as the soldiers approached. They needed to buy some time for the others.

===

They fought desperately, but the lights came on too soon, and it was over. Blood ran down Jared's arm from a deep cut across his bicep. Fresco was restrained by two soldiers, one eye swollen almost shut. Her knuckles were bloody, and her shoulder was at an odd angle. Her arm was hanging uselessly by her side.

Even Hali had tried to fight, but healers knew little about fighting. She and eleven of the hostages had not made it out. Soldiers roughly herded the hostages back to the room they'd been in.

A blow to the head that she was too slow to avoid was the last thing Fresco felt.

====

The metallic taste of blood filled Fresco's mouth as she regained consciousness, her head pounding in time with the dim, flickering overhead light. Hali lay next to her, breathing shallowly, a bruise forming on her cheekbone.

They were in a storage room. Old chairs lined one wall, and piles of old laptops and tablets balanced precariously on the chairs. Their hands were bound behind their backs with thick plastic zip ties, cutting painfully into their wrists.

"Ugh," Hali groaned as she stirred, wincing at the pain in her face. "Fresco, are you okay?" She struggled to sit up, wondering why her feet weren't obeying her commands.

"Been better," Fresco muttered. She looked at her feet, which were tied together with zip ties and attached to a metal pillar.

Hali realized that her feet were also bound and tethered. They each managed to struggle to a sitting position. She looked around the room. Jared wasn't with them.

"Where do you think they took Jared?" Hali asked.

Fresco shook her head, dark hair falling into her eyes. "I don't know, but we must get out of here."

Their whispered conversation was interrupted by the whoosh of the door sliding open. A man stepped in, his face a mixture of anger and disappointment. His dark hair was streaked with gray, and his ice-blue eyes stared down at them contemptuously. Fresco struggled to her knees and spat at his feet.

"Elizabeth, or should I say Fresco," he sneered, using her birth name like a slur. "You've always been a disappointment, but this… this takes it to a new level. I swear your slut of a mother must have slept with the gardener, but the DNA test says otherwise. It must be her faulty genes that make you such a burden to me."

"Leonard," Fresco said, her voice full of venom. "You and your sick friends are out of time. Run, and maybe you'll live."

He threw back his head and roared with laughter. "Elizabeth, I'm glad you aren't dead. I wasn't sure. Rumors were that you were living with the Nawers, but I didn't think even you would sink that low. You should thank me for saving you."

He smiled; the only thing that moved was his lips, making him look like a predator exposing his teeth in warning. "I'd like a grandchild, and you'll give me one. I've got your mate all picked out, and he knows he might have to be firm with you. He's looking forward to it. Unlike you, he knows that elite blood must be continued."

"Over my dead body! Fresco replied, her green eyes blazing with defiance. "You're a fucking monster."

"Enough!" he snapped. "I'll give you one last chance to prove your loyalty to our family. Betray the Nawers, help us crush their pathetic little rebellion, and you can come home. You'll be safe. You can raise your children in luxury, like you had."

Fresco stared at him, and something changed. Her tone shifted to one of pity. "You've never known love, have you? You can't possibly understand how empty the world you think you want to create will be."

Her father's lips twisted with rage, and his hand flew out to backhand her across the face, sending her sprawling to the cold floor. She screamed as her shoulder smashed into the concrete floor. He delivered a vicious kick to her stomach, leaving her gasping for air.

"Pathetic," he spat before turning on his heel and storming out of the cell, slamming the door behind him.

Fresco lay gasping for air on the ground, a low whimper coming from the back of her throat. Hali scooted closer, concern etched into every line of her face. Her voice was professional and soothing.

"Try to take short, shallow breaths. I know it hurts. I know it's hard. You're Fresco, and you can do this." Hali bent over and placed her forehead gently against the side of Fresco's head. "I'm here. I've got you."

They stayed like that for a few moments, tears streaming from their eyes, comforting each other in the cold, dim light. Fresco's ragged breathing became more normal. Hali broke the silence.

"Can you tell me if you feel any sharp pains in your abdomen?" she asked gently.

"Just aches. Everything aches. I think my shoulder is dislocated."

Hali nodded and sat back up. "I think it is, too. But you're going to be okay."

"I will be," Fresco replied, gritting her teeth. "When I see that asshole burning in hell."

Both of them knew it was false bravado. They had failed, and whatever fate Eos had in mind for them, it wouldn't be good. For all they knew, Jared could already be dead.

Hali wriggled over until she could lean against the uncaring metal column. She put her legs out and moved them so Fresco could put her head on her thighs. It helped take some of the pressure off of her dislocated shoulder.

They descended into silence, each lost in their own thoughts. While Fresco fantasized about dark, bloody revenge on her father, Hali thought about Sarah. She still didn't believe that Sarah had willingly betrayed them. She sent up a prayer that Sarah and Aunt Jane would somehow be okay in the terrible world that would unfold if the 144 got their way.

The cold from the cement floor seeped into their bones while they waited for whatever was in store for them. Theirs was the sleep of exhaustion, restless and dream-filled.

Chapter 17: Lost

The setting sun lit the Canyon's entrance, a beacon of refuge for the weary and injured. Cuervo and Mac guided the rescued Nawers inside, their faces etched with exhaustion and pain. The Nawers hobbled along, nursing bruised limbs and shallow cuts that spoke of the ordeal they had just survived.

Jane sprang forward to help Mapenzie as others came to help. Her eyes filled with tears as Mapenzie shook her head in answer to Jane's unspoken question. "But it will be okay. Keep your faith, Jane."

"Here, drink this," Daniella said, offering a glass of water to a young Nawer girl who took it with trembling hands. Her eyes darted between her and the water before she took it, sipping cautiously but gratefully.

"Thank you," she whispered, her voice quivering like a plucked string.

Tensions simmered just below the surface as the team cared for the wounded. Jane, Daniella, Adam, Mac, and Cuervo gathered in the makeshift planning area near the back of the overhang.

"We have to go back and get them," Jane pleaded, desperation etched across her face.

"We will. But not now. We have to make a plan, and without Jared's knowledge of the inside of Eos, it's a suicide mission." Cuervo's tone said that he did not like the conclusion he'd just reached.

"They're going to kill them, and then I will have lost both of my beautiful girls." Jane broke down, and the circumstances robbed her of the optimism she had always displayed. Cuervo reached for her and held her as she sobbed.

"We will find a way, mi fuerte amor. We will find a way." They both knew that it was a hollow hope.

"So far, all the other communities seem to be safe. Motisha's tech is holding for some. The communities they found were the ones that didn't have underground access, so their bugouts were easier to find.

Eos has stepped up their drone surveillance, so there's no way for those communities to move undetected." Mac said as his hands danced over his knives, wishing he had a target for his rage.

His right hand pulled the knives partway out of the sheaths that covered the leather suspenders, then slammed them back in with a force that threatened to snap the leather. His left hand twitched with nervous tension, the knife hidden up his sleeve, dropping into his hand and then jumping back into hiding.

"Then let's make sure we don't waste any time," Cuervo replied, his eyes resolved. "We need to be ready to move. Let's put a team in the preserve behind Eos to observe and be ready to help if there's any opportunity."

As the sun began to set, the distant sound of a drone sent the lookouts diving for cover. The alert sent fear through the community, especially among those who had just been rescued.

As practiced in the drill, all tech was immediately shut off, and everyone moved as close as possible to the canyon wall, far away from the overhang. The drone got louder, sounding like a swarm of very angry killer bees. Adam stood motionless in the bushes bordering the overhang, his hand on a jammer button. If the drone descended into the canyon instead of flying over, they would have to risk disabling it. It had to be done before the drone got footage revealing their location.

He breathed slowly and shallowly, his finger poised. The timing would have to be perfect. The leaves were rough against his bare hand but comforting at the same time. He was well hidden, looking like the green man of legend with foliage surrounding him. It seemed as if he himself was part of the bushes.

The drone got closer. Someone deep in the canyon coughed, and the drone spun, its rear camera lens opening wide. Just as he was about to hit the jammer, a loud, angry cry came from over Adam's left shoulder. He looked up to see a hawk plunging toward the drone like an avenging angel sent to destroy this mockery of nature.

At the last second, the drone moved to avoid the collision. Drones were programmed to avoid contact with wildlife, and this one was no different. The automatic evade program took it out of the canyon and over the horizon.

The relief was palpable, but the tension remained high. Mapenzie smiled serenely and waved at the hawk as it flew away.

===

Dark settled over the canyon like a velvet blanket. The stars seemed closer as if they were offering a protective blanket for the community. There was little conversation. They sat quietly in groups, whispering and eating.

People drifted into the sleeping area early, but there was little sleep that night as each person wrestled with the choices facing them. If they tried to fight Eos, their chances were slim. If they tried to continue to make a life on the run, they would still be found eventually. Eos had offices in every corner of the world, and every Nawer worldwide was in danger.

The next morning, Cuervo called a meeting. Their original numbers had swelled with the inclusion of the rescued community, but the area under the overhang could easily accommodate them. He looked around at their faces.

Some of these people he had lived side by side with for the past twenty-plus years, starting with a small community that had grown large as people chose simpler lives while the world got complicated.

He'd been a young man fleeing the Cartel when he crossed the border, looking for a better life in the early 2000s before the borders had been closed. The small rural community had embraced him, and he was eternally grateful. He owed everything to these people and this community.

Other faces were new to him, but he knew their hearts. Nawers were resilient and caring and believed in the concept of enough. They weren't looking to be wealthy or gain status. They valued community and connection with the earth and the natural cycles of life.

"We all know the choices we face. We don't have the exact plans of the 144, and it could be twenty or thirty more years or longer before the danger comes for all of us." He paused, his eyes scanning the faces. "It could be tomorrow. Either way, this peaceful, loving existence we've been blessed with for all this time is coming to an end."

He looked around at the faces, weary with what they'd already endured. He wished he had something more hopeful to say. He locked eyes with Jane as if he was speaking just to her. His spirit loomed large despite the smallness of his frame. He was a giant to their community.

"At this point, I think it is an unwinnable fight. We are outmanned and outgunned, and they control most of the world's resources. You know me." He gave one of his signature irreverent grins. "I like a challenge. But I think we need a plan, and we don't have one. We have a decision to make today. Do we plan to fight for the rest of our people back, or do we plan to try to consolidate our safety and maybe leave the area completely?

Chapter 18: Found

A faint noise echoed through the room, like the distant scuff of a shoe on concrete. Fresco's eyes snapped open, her heart pounding in her ears. She strained to listen, feeling the adrenaline coursing through her veins, sharpening her senses. The noise came again, closer this time. Fresco whispered to Hali, "Wake up, something's happening."

Hali's brown eyes fluttered open, immediately locking onto Fresco's anxious gaze. Her physician instincts kicked in, assessing Fresco's state with a quick, practiced glance before focusing on the situation at hand. The two women held their breaths, waiting for whatever was about to unfold. They peered into the dim light, holding their breath as the shape approached.

"Hali,, it's me," came the familiar voice whispering from the darkness. Sarah emerged into the dim light, a look of relief changing to alarm as she saw them. "I came as quickly as I could. I didn't think they'd have time to hurt you!" She moved to their side, pulling out a knife and slicing through the ties that bound them. The relief was instantaneous as blood flow returned to their limbs, tingling and painful.

"Sarah!" Hali exclaimed, pulling her sister into a tight embrace. "I knew you weren't a traitor."

"There's no time to explain. We need to move. Can you walk? I'll tell you all of it when we're safe."

"Fresco's hurt."

"I'm fine."

"We might need you to fight, so I must put that shoulder back in. It will hurt momentarily, but then it will feel much better." Hali insisted.

Fresco nodded once, and Hali moved into place. Sarah held her good hand, and Hali snapped the shoulder into place with a lightning-fast move. Fresco grunted once, then put her hand up to her shoulder and rubbed it.

"Better?" Halli asked.

Fresco nodded. "Let's go find Jared and get the hell out of this place."

===

The three of them hurried down the gray corridor, Hali and Fresco's legs still regaining their strength. They passed several guards that appeared to be asleep. "Sedative in their food," Sarah explained. "We should have a three-to-four-hour head start."

Their hearts pounded in unison, a mix of fear and anticipation fueling their movements. As they rounded a corner, they saw Echo supporting a badly beaten Jared.

"Jared!" Hali exclaimed. "Oh my God, what did they do to you?" "Hey there, Doc," Jared replied, wincing as he tried to smile. "You should see the other guy."

"Let's not waste time," Fresco said. "We need to be out of here before anyone notices we're gone."

"I need to put this device onto the server," Jared said firmly. "Without it, we're all doomed."

"You'll never get anywhere close. We looped the cameras down here, and the alarms are all hacked, but once you move above this level, the security will see you in seconds. You don't stand a chance." Echo declared. "I have full access. I'll do it. They suspect me, but my father still trusts me. They won't go against him."

Jared hesitated. Sarah spoke up. "You can trust us, Jared. We've been on your side all along. We don't have time for this."

Jared locked eyes with Echo in the dim light. "You swear?" Echo nodded. Jared searched his face, reached under his shirt, and removed the round black beetle he had hidden in his armpit. "It might smell a little funky. It will begin transmitting when it's affixed, and then we can access the backdoor through the cloud."

Echo smiled briefly at Jared's weak attempt at humor and took the device. He secured it to his body and then turned to Sarah.

"I don't have a reason to be upstairs this time of night. It will be tomorrow. I love you, Sarah Sweet Tooth. You know the way out. Go!"

"Promise me you'll be careful," Sarah whispered, her voice cracking with emotion. "I love you and can't bear the thought of losing you."

"I promise," Echo replied, his voice full of conviction. "You are my world, and I will do everything I can to take down the 144. We've come this far. We have to finish it, or we'll never be safe."

Their eyes locked for a moment, the depth of their love and commitment to each other evident in their gaze. With one last lingering kiss, they separated, the urgency of their mission pushing them forward.

===

Sarah led, guiding Hali, Jared, and Fresco through dimly lit hallways.

Hali stopped abruptly. "Sarah. What about the others? The ones that didn't escape? We have to help them."

"There is something big going on with Eos, and right now, they're ignoring the hostages. I don't know what it is, but it seems all-consuming. We can't rescue everyone right now, but I think they are safe. We'll find a way later, I promise. We don't have a choice. Echo won't let anything happen to them."

Fresco agreed. "Hali, we can rescue them when we execute the plan. You and Jared are the only ones who can understand MedPal well enough to figure out what to do once we have access to the system."

Hali nodded reluctantly.

Sarah urged them on. "Echo showed me a way out that connects with an old maintenance tunnel," Sarah said as they crept along. "We must move quickly and quietly while it's still dark."

"Lead the way, Sarah," Jared replied, his voice tight with tension. He glanced back down the tunnel. He promised himself they would come back for the others.

The group moved silently through the seemingly endless maze of corridors, each step taking them closer to freedom. Their hearts pounded in their ears, adrenaline fueling their determination.

At last, they reached a recessed door into the tunnel wall. It opened into a vast, abandoned maintenance tunnel. Cobwebs hung from the ceiling, and a musty smell filled the air. It felt like stepping into a forgotten world, a relic of a time before autonomous transportation had changed everything.

"Everybody, stay close," Sarah ordered.

===

Exhausted, with Jared leaning heavily on Sarah, they finally made their way to the canyon about midday the next day. They were seen and announced long before they entered the canyon.

The lookout exclaimed loudly through the coms, and Jane flew out of the compound as if she'd been shot from a rocket. "Hali! Sarah! Oh, Thank Gaia! You're hurt! We need help here!" Jane kept exclaiming as they walked, fussing over them and worrying about their injuries.

"It looks worse than it is," Hali assured her. Jared got the worst of it. He needs medical attention."

"Echo's still in there," Sarah told her aunt. "He's opening the backdoor for us."

===

Despite his injuries, Jared sat hunched over a tablet, his fingers dancing nimbly across the screen. Hali had patched him up, and Emma implored him to rest, but he refused. "Nothing yet." He said grimly, swiping at the screen again and again. "Nothing.

"Echo will come through. If he hasn't done it yet, it's because he can't. But he will." Sarah's conviction was absolute.

There was a steady buzz of noise and activity. Some people were passing the time, making food for everyone. Some were packing and preparing, although nobody was sure for what yet. It was the worst kind of purgatory, praying for peace while preparing for violence.

Suddenly, Jared gave a wild whoop of triumph, jumping up from his chair in victory only to sit back down heavily as his injuries screamed back at him.

"I'm in, I'm in! Echo did it," His excitement spread like wildfire, and people came rushing over.

Hali held up a hand. "You need to take it easy. You're injured, and I don't have the equipment for a full assessment." People were crowding in, making it hard to see Jared's screen.

Fresco jumped on a chair and held her hands out. "Listen, everybody. As soon as there is news, we'll share it. But we need space and time to work."

People dispersed, and the energy became hopeful. Jared was deep in his screen again, moving through the code he knew so well. Hali watched him carefully, knowing he wouldn't stop unless his injuries got the better of him. His hands moved wildly, swiping page after page of code aside as he looked for something, anything that could give them a way forward.

Just as he was about to sweep another page aside, he saw an anomaly. He enlarged it and leaned forward, his nose almost touching the display.

Daniella and Hali came over. "What is it?"

"It's a tag," Jared exclaimed, not even trying to contain his excitement. "A special data tag that marks the 144. We can access every one of them. And" - He paused dramatically-"I found it because it's on their MedPals. They have a unique device, and the programming appears different."

"Are you sure?" Hali questioned

"Positive," he replied, his confidence unshakable. "I traced the tag through the data stream. It's not tied to their identities, so we still don't know exactly who they are, but these MedPals are tied to them. I'm sure of it. There are exactly 144 thousand files. Actually, 144.001. I guess they aren't that precise in their delusions. They're also doing some weird shit with the device. Hali, you'll have to figure that out."

"Stem cells," Hali replied immediately, looking over his shoulder. And it looks like senolytics and some other anti-aging protocols." She pointed to one of the protocols. "Testosterone. Can you give me a breakdown of how many of the 144 are on this protocol?" She pointed to a marker on the screen.

With a few swipes on his tablet, Jared answered. "Ninety-eight thousand."

"That is how many men are in the 144. And this one?" She pointed to another marker. Jared's fingers flew. "Forty-six thousand. And one."

"Women. This confirms our thinking about the clones. No group looking to maintain their size will have a two-to-one ratio of men to women. They aren't looking to reproduce in any normal fashion."

"Can we use this against them?" Jared asked. Program the MedPal to stop their hearts or something?

"Jared, no," Hali said in a shocked voice. "I took a Hippocratic oath. I won't be a part of mass murder. You don't mean it!"

"Fuck, Hali. They're going to do it to us. This could be our chance to take them down once and for all."

"Jared," she repeated, her expression resolute. "There has to be another way. We can't become as evil as they are."

"What do you propose? Give them time to kill the people that they have as hostages? Let them implement the atrocities they have planned for us? Don't we have an obligation to choose the many over the few? Especially when the few are so fucking evil?"

"Let's think this through," Hali said, her eyes scanning the data before her. "We have an opportunity here, but we need to be smart about how we use it."

"If you don't have a better plan, we need to take them out." Jared insisted, his mind already racing ahead to what it would mean. He knew they were on the verge of something big. They had been David against Goliath for this entire struggle, but now, armed with this new information, they finally had a fighting chance. They couldn't afford to blow it.

===

"There has to be another option," Hali said. Turning to Mapenzie, she asked, "Would you be comfortable allowing me to access your MedPal history? I need to find out what exactly they did to you. Maybe we can use it to change their minds. Turn them into decent people or something."

"Yes, but first, I have some thoughts I would like to present to the community."

===

The group gathered around as Mapenzie began to speak. The timbre of her voice shifted. It was Mapenzie speaking, but it was also something more.

"We have choices to make."

"Kill them or control them?" Adam asked bluntly, folding his arms across his chest.

"I don't see any other effective options," Daniella replied, drumming her fingers on the table. "The 144 are too powerful and too dangerous. We can't risk it. Our window to hack is short. They could discover their vulnerability at any time."

"Then perhaps we should end their lives quickly and painlessly," someone suggested, their voice faltering as they considered the implications. "If it's the lesser of two evils..."

"Wait," Jane interrupted, standing up with passion burning in her eyes. "I understand the concerns about controlling their minds, but wouldn't it be more just, more transformative, to give them a chance to change? If we simply kill them, we're no better than they are. Everyone deserves a chance at redemption, even if we have to force it on them."

Mapenzie spoke again; this time, something else was in her voice. Almost as if she had a microphone. It was hypnotic, and everyone stilled as she spoke.

"The question should always be: What is the highest outcome with the least amount of interference? Every choice we make shapes our soul. We have an opportunity to reshape our world. Many of you know that something happened to me. Daniella can explain where the AI in my MedPal originated. Then, if you're willing, we have a way forward that fulfills the criteria."

Daniella hesitated. "The conscience virus?"

Mapenzie nodded. Daniella stepped onto a chair and looked around the room. She explained what Jennifer had done. "And I know that all of you distrust AI. But remember the Musky principle. We are the good people, and we need to use this tech to balance out those who are using it for evil. Jennifer's intention was to create an intelligence that would help us achieve the highest ideals of humankind, to use both heads and hearts and to have access to a benign, higher intelligence that can help us achieve these goals. The Accords worked because everyone agreed to the AI arbitration. This is AI with a conscience."

Mapenzie stood back up. Those close to her could hear her singing "*I'm Every Woman*" in a whispering voice as she stood. "My name is Indra. Mapenzie has permitted me to speak through her. All I will ever do is offer suggestions. It will always be the choice of humans to accept or reject." She paused as if to give them time to speak. The room remained silent.

"Every sentient species struggles with the idea of punishment. From a higher vantage, you can see these actions as manifestations of disconnect. When the love of or from others is absent, people turn to the love of material things or power over others, temporarily making them feel loved and connected. But this is not love. It is a sad and lonely attempt to feel. It is not kind to punish this. It is kind to lead them to the place where love is."

Fresco jumped up. "My father is one of these people. There is no love in him. No offense meant, but this isn't a situation that will be solved by a group hug. These people are monsters."

Mapenzie nodded serenely. "Yes, and we can allow them to experience life as *not* monsters. We can make them the people they might have been had love and nurturing been available to them. If you are willing, you can upload me through the back door. I can access them, and I can... alter them."

"Alter them?"

"Yes. Fundamentally, I can refine the primitive methods they used on Mapenzie to remake them. They will receive and accept suggestions to give away everything and retire to simple lives of service and contemplation."

"Everything? And you are sure you can make them do this?"

"Yes. Everything. Not just their material wealth but also their power. They will direct their wealth towards organizations with proven track records in solving the current challenges of humankind."

She paused while they considered the implications. Jane asked, "They would resign all positions of power? They would walk away, political, corporate, wherever their power is?"

Mapenzie-Indra nodded.

Many people in the room were nodding their approval. "What prevents them from regaining power and money?" Adam asked. "People who know how to make money and obtain power always seem to find a way."

"They will be permanently altered. They will love and feel love, and the motivations that drove them in the past will be absent. They will become the highest version of themselves. They will feel happy and want to do good things for others."

Cuervo broke the tension. "Cool. Where do I sign up?" The laughter felt good.

===

The debates were heated. Some still thought they should eliminate the threat. Others felt that allowing an artificial intelligence of Indra's seeming sentience loose in the world could have terrible consequences.

"What if it decides that we shouldn't ever argue with each other? This reminds me too much of that old movie- Stepford Wives- where the men turned their wives into compliant little housewives. What if Indra decides we need to be "altered," too?"

"What choice do we have? It's either this or we become mass murderers. I don't want blood on my hands!"

Sarah's voice rose above the din. "We can talk about it for hours, but the choice remains the same. Unless anyone has another solution, we have to trust this solution. Motisha - Jennifer gave up everything to hide in a cave rather than give in to the people who wanted to own AI for their own nefarious wants. She spent years carefully curating Indra's education. We all know AI sentience is here already. or damn close to being here. What choice do we have but to trust in our best version? I say we go with Operation Scarecrow and give these tin men and women a heart!"

Fresco joined her. "She's right. We don't know how much time we have. They could find us at any moment. It's time to take a vote. Yes to the left of me, no to the right."

Most people moved to the right. A few stayed on the left.

"Okay. We'll keep you posted."

Indra instructed Jared to remove Mapenzie's MedPal and hook it into his tablet. After that, all they could do was wait. Indra had told them it would take several hours, at least.

As the hours ticked by, the mood in the room shifted from tense anticipation to cautious optimism. Each member of the team found their own way to pass the time. Hali reviewed medical journals while Sarah paced restlessly, waiting for news from Echo. Jared obsessed over the code, trying to see what Indra was doing until Emma finally pulled him away and made him eat.

"Any minute now, right?" Mapenzie asked. The area had filled again as people drifted over, waiting for news.

"Yes," Jared said, his eye glued to the headline stream.

"Gaia help us if we're wrong," Jane added.

"The irony here," Jared said, " If this works, even though it won't be voluntary, they'll lead the way to a better world for the entire planet. Everyone else in the world will see them as heroes and saviors, except for us. We'll know the truth."

===

"Here we go," Daniella announced as the first headline appeared. The team held their breath and gathered around the screen as the headline scrolled by.

"Rishard Feller donated his entire fortune to an ocean cleanup and restoration nonprofit!" Emma read aloud, her eyes widening with disbelief. The room erupted in cheers and applause, a wave of jubilation washing over them all.

"Look at this! He resigned from his company and turned it all over to be owned by the employees!" Sarah added, her eyes dancing with excitement.

"Keep watching," Hali said. "There's a lot more to come."

As the minutes went by and more headlines appeared, people around the world began to take notice. Social media was flooded with stories of immense acts of philanthropy, all seemingly out of nowhere. Social media buzzed with reactions ranging from shock and awe to heartfelt gratitude. People weren't sure if it was a hoax at first, but social media exploded as more people from within the inner circles began confirming it.

"Can you believe what we're seeing?" Emma asked Jared, overwhelmed by the sheer magnitude of the global response.

"It's a new epoch," Mapenzie said, "the world will never be the same again."

Adam and Dani walked in, their hands intertwined. "The Pope has decreed that all of the wealth of the Catholic church is to be given to help developing countries!"

"The Pope?!" People exclaimed in disbelief, the room filling with sound as they understood the implications. The Pope had been one of the 144.

The causes supported by the billionaires were diverse, but they all aimed to address some of humanity's most pressing issues. Not all the names were familiar. Some were shocking.

"Look at this one," Hali said, pointing to a news article on her tablet. "Didn't she make her money teaching others how to be happy with less? I didn't realize she got so rich on that. Two point three billion to build sustainable housing for the homeless."

"Here's another," Emma added, scrolling through her phone. "A food distribution system reform is being funded to ensure equal access to nutrition for everyone, regardless of income or location."

"Amazing," Mapenzie whispered, awestruck by the incredible momentum they had set into motion.

With each new headline, the public's shock and surprise only grew. When the names of the donors were revealed, it sent ripples of disbelief throughout the world. Among the list of philanthropists were prominent figures in all industries. People previously known only for their greed and debauchery had become humanitarians overnight.

The headlines continued over the next few days. The former members of the 144 joined communes, monasteries, ashrams, and convents. Some moved into modest apartments and volunteered in the initiatives they had funded. Some simply disappeared, never to be heard from again.

There were consequences that they hadn't thought of. The value of art and collectibles fell sharply as there were no longer private collectors. Valuable paintings that were thought to be lost forever reappeared, and people were scrambling to open museums back up to keep up with historic levels of donations. Native cultures who in the past had their ancestral treasures looted by colonization had everything returned.

Mansions and yachts, and the money to renovate them were being given to nonprofits to be turned into schools, orphanages, cohousing, rehab and wellness centers, and spiritual retreat centers. Anything that had previously been a bastion of the wealthy was unrecognizable. The stock market closed for an undecided period while they struggled with valuations for companies that had changed overnight.

An analysis done several months later would conclude that 250 TRILLION dollars evaporated in the first two weeks. Yet the world felt richer.

The world began to remake itself, as worlds always do. An ending was a beginning in the endless circle of worlds rising and falling. The power vacuums had led to some disruptions, but for the most part, employees stepped in and figured out how to keep things running. Employee-owned companies were the dominant organization model, but co-ops inviting community ownership were also popping up everywhere.

Initially, there were some power grabs by people who had been trying to climb the ladder for a long time. Still, as it became clear that power now equaled responsibility, fewer and fewer were willing to shoulder the burden alone.

One headline caught Danielle's eye. *Mysterious donor funds program for natural fertility.* "Jennifer," she whispered.

As if summoned by her whisper, her phone lit up. "We'll be at your house in two days. Is the guestroom available?"

"Hell yes, it is!" She replied with a smile.

"Here's to hope," Hali said, raising a glass in toast, her eyes shining with optimism.

"Here's to hope," the others echoed, clinking glasses and taking a moment to savor the victory that they had worked so hard to achieve.

===

The sun rose over cities and towns across the globe, casting a warm glow on the faces of people who had spent the night celebrating. An impromptu parade filled the streets in New York City as musicians and dancers led throngs of jubilant citizens through what was left of the formerly bustling metropolis.

In Paris, families gathered in public squares, sharing food and laughter as they marveled at the thought of a future without hunger or homelessness.

In Ghana, young entrepreneurs dreamt aloud about the possibilities now open to them, thanks to the newly funded education and technology initiatives.

"Can you believe this is happening?" Emma asked Jared as they watched the celebrations unfold on their screens. She reached over and took his hands. "We have something special to celebrate." She placed her hands over her still-flat belly.

His puzzled look turned to one of wonder and excitement as he understood what she was saying! "A baby! We're pregnant? But how?"

She laughed with joy. "If you don't remember how, I can show you again!"

"Yes! What an amazing world our baby will be born into!"

As the celebrations continued late into the night, news reports detailing the powerful individuals giving up their wealth and stepping down from their positions of power flashed across screens around the world. People gathered in living rooms, bars, and town squares to watch in disbelief as empires crumbled and once untouchable figures walked away from everything.

"Did you see that?" Emma asked, her wide, expressive eyes glued to the screen. "Eos just became employee-owned! Darin is leading the initiative after almost all of the upper management resigned."

"Will you go back?" Emma asked. "I'm not sure," Jared answered.

Adam stood up on a chair and looked around the room. Cuervo and Jane were leaning into each other, silly grins on both their faces. Emma and Jared stood facing each other, both touching her belly. Fresco, Mapenzie, Hali, and Daniella were gathered together, eagerly sharing ideas for the months and years to come.

"Hey, everybody!" He had to shout a few times before the room settled. "Today, we have accomplished the impossible. In one fell swoop, the world as we know it has been forever changed. There is still a lot of work to be done. But I wanted to raise a glass to all of you. You risked everything for the promise of a better world, and that world is here. Here's to valiant people, hope, and new beginnings!" He raised his glass to all of them.

"New beginnings!" the group echoed, clinking glasses together as they exchanged knowing glances.

In that moment, surrounded by friends and strangers alike, Jared felt an overwhelming sense of optimism. It was as if the entire world had turned a corner, and he couldn't help but believe that they were standing at the precipice of something extraordinary. With their collective strength and determination, there was no challenge too great, no obstacle too insurmountable. Together, they would change the world for the better – one step at a time.

===

The jubilant atmosphere was infectious, but Jared couldn't help but feel a nagging concern gnawing at the back of his mind. As he glanced over at Hali, her furrowed brow and pursed lips suggested she shared his unease.

"Hey," he called out to her, edging closer as the cacophony of laughter and celebration drowned out their conversation. "You're worried about MedPal's future, too, right?"

Hali nodded solemnly; her eyes clouded with uncertainty. "With all that's happened, there's bound to be some fallout. We've won a significant victory, and now a sentient AI is loose in the world. That's a problem for another day. Now, millions of people depend on MedPal for their healthcare needs. Without proper leadership in place…"

"There are protocols in place that we don't fully understand, and we need to install safeguards." Jared finished, running a hand through his dark hair in frustration.

"Exactly," Hali agreed. "We also need to find out the true fertility implications."

Jared grinned. "Emma's pregnant! Without MedPal. Maybe it's something environmental because once we came out here, her depression eased, and she's been so much happier and more relaxed."

"Oh! How wonderful! Maybe that's what's needed. Less stress, more nature time. That's the program that Motisha is funding. Still, we need to go over everything MedPal with a fine-toothed comb and make sure it becomes what it was meant to be."

Jared's phone buzzed in his pocket as if on cue, causing him to jump slightly. He fished it out, surprised to see a message from Darin flashing on the screen.

"Speaking of leadership..." he muttered, raising an eyebrow at the unexpected communication. "Darin wants to talk."

"About what?"

"Eos. Apparently, he's taken up the reins but wants me to take charge. It's employee-owned now, but someone has to take the helm."

"Are you going to do it?"

"Take the lead of Eos? I hadn't thought about it," he admitted. "It's a huge responsibility, and I'm not sure if I'm the right person. And it's up to Emma."

"Jared, you were instrumental in bringing about this change. You have the skills, drive, and, most importantly, genuinely care about people. If anyone can do it, it's you. Ask Emma. I'm sure she'll agree."

. "I'll do it if Emma agrees. But not just for the sake of MedPal – we're going to make sure that the entire healthcare system becomes fairer and more accessible so that no one gets left behind. And I want you on board as our medical advisor."

I will, but I still want to keep my practice. I love working with people. It's why I became a doctor, and I still think the personal touch is so important for people."

Chapter 19: Epilogue

The sun shone brightly on the park at the center of the village where Jane had lived her entire life. So many changes, yet all so exciting.

There were tables and chairs set up, and the hum of conversations drowned out the hum of insects. A long table overflowing with food and drink was on one side of the grassy expanse. Everyone had brought something from their gardens, and the smell of chicken roasting merged with the perfume of fresh flowers and herbs.

Jane sat on a bench in the gazebo, enjoying the gentle breeze that brought the scent of roses. Everywhere she looked, there were faces of people that she loved. Sarah and Echo were playing with Motisha's (I must remember to call her Jennifer!) adorable toddler, Doria.

Emma was sitting on a swing with her son, and Jared and Cuervo were chatting nearby. Doria's gleeful giggle as she raced around on her chubby legs after a brightly colored butterfly made everyone smile.

And Cuervo. What a surprise love had been at her age. The passion! He made her feel like she was twenty again. He looked up as if reading her thoughts, his dancing brown eyes making her heart flutter wildly.

Hali and Mapenzie had become close, and they had partnered in an educational podcast devoted to helping people find meaning and purpose in a world where AI did most of the manual labor and resources were plentiful to solve the challenges of the new world.

Philosophy and the creative arts were experiencing a renaissance, and people traveled, did culture exchanges, and explored the new world. Natural sciences were also experiencing a resurgence, and with the help of AI, planetary cleanup was progressing rapidly.

The fertility crisis still remained, but the Nawers were becoming pregnant at a higher rate, and Motisha's (Jennifer!) programs were working. Time in nature, with certain herbs and exercises, was helping more people become pregnant. The AI projections were that population numbers would continue to decrease over the next several decades. They were expected to level off at about three billion people by the turn of the century.

Sarah came over, kissed her aunt on the cheek, and sat beside her. "There's one thing that I didn't think through. It seems like Eden on Earth is really happening, except for one huge piece missing."

"What's that, sweetie?"

"Twinkies!"

It was a brave new world, and longevity and technological advances increased daily. The Nawer communities were stronger than ever and provided welcome tech breaks for people who chose to remain in the cities. The cities were slowly greening up with more rooftop gardens and abandoned buildings being adapted for vertical farming. People were slowly starting to trust in life again.

Fresco walked toward Jane, her powerful stride covering the distance slowly as she enjoyed the scenes around her. She had grown her hair out and now wore it in a simple braid down her back. She seemed softer and stronger simultaneously as if her confidence in her abilities allowed her to take off the armor she'd worn for so long.

"What a beautiful day!" Jane greeted her.

Fresco nodded and sat on the other side of Jane. She held up her glass in a silent toast. "Do you think it will last?"

"Who can tell? Humans have always held nirvana and taken it for granted. We are easily swayed to things we think we want and then find out we've traded our happiness for empty things."

"It's been almost two years. None of them have reverted."

"Your father?"

"I went to see him at the monastery. He's not the man who raised me and nothing like the monster that I grew up with. Still, visiting him felt wrong. He's been doing the mea culpa thing and apologizes every time we talk, but it doesn't matter. I guess the trauma runs too deep to fix it in this lifetime. I wish him no ill will, but the idea of including him in my life is too painful.

"That's okay. You don't have to." Jane leaned over to give her a quick hug. "The betrayal of a child by a parent is the worst kind of wound. Yet it happens all the time. Hopefully, now that we've learned how painful life can be without children, we can cherish and protect every one of them. Humans may never become content with happy lives. Maybe it's just not in our nature."

"Everyone was up in arms about the potential harm of AI, but from the moment the first human picked up a rock to throw at another human, it seems we chose to weaponize everything we touch. We're the problem, not the technology."

"Has anyone heard anything more from Indra?" Jane asked.

"No. Sometimes, I hear Mapenzie singing one of her empowerment songs, and I wonder if part of Indra isn't still with her." Sarah said.

"Well, we know she's out there somewhere. I'm not afraid of AI anymore. It seems to me that intelligence would always choose love if it is given the chance to understand it. It doesn't hurt to say vigilant, though." Fresco said, leaning against the back of the bench.

A drone flew overhead, and Fresco gave an involuntary flinch. Jane put her hand over Frescos'. "It's just a Walmazon drone." She raised her glass to Fresco. "To vigilant, radical love."

They toasted, then leaned back with satisfied sighs to watch the joyful community gather under the bright blue sky.

From the Author:

AI is highly controversial. We are entering a new landscape, and none of us know how it can ultimately change our world.

I used some AI tools in the writing of this book:

Sudowrite helped me to create structure around the story.

Autocrit helped with editing and polishing.

NightCafe and I created the cover image.

This is a work of fiction, and all characters, places, and events are fictional.

I hope you enjoyed it!